# MATED IN DARKNESS

## A TALON PACK NOVEL

## CARRIE ANN RYAN

# MATED IN DARKNESS

A Talon Pack Novel
By Carrie Ann Ryan

Mated in Darkness
A Talon Pack Novel
By: Carrie Ann Ryan
© 2021 Carrie Ann Ryan
eBook ISBN: 978-1-63695-215-4
Paperback ISBN: 978-1-63695-198-0

Cover Art by Sweet N Spicy Designs

*For my readers.*
*Long Live The Pack!*

"Count on Carrie Ann Ryan for emotional, sexy, character driven stories that capture your heart!" – Carly Phillips, NY Times bestselling author

"Carrie Ann Ryan's romances are my newest addiction! The emotion in her books captures me from the very beginning. The hope and healing hold me close until the end. These love stories will simply sweep you away." ~ NYT Bestselling Author Deveny Perry

"Carrie Ann Ryan writes the perfect balance of sweet and heat ensuring every story feeds the soul." - Audrey Carlan, #1 New York Times Bestselling Author

"Carrie Ann Ryan never fails to draw readers in with passion, raw sensuality, and characters that pop off the page. Any book by Carrie Ann is an absolute treat." – New York Times Bestselling Author J. Kenner

"Carrie Ann Ryan knows how to pull your heartstrings and make your pulse pound! Her wonderful Redwood Pack series will draw you in and keep you reading long into the night. I can't wait to see what comes next with the new generation, the Talons. Keep them coming, Carrie Ann!" –Lara Adrian, New York Times bestselling author of CRAVE THE NIGHT

"With snarky humor, sizzling love scenes, and brilliant, imaginative worldbuilding, The Dante's Circle series reads as if Carrie Ann Ryan peeked at my personal wish list!" – NYT Bestselling Author, Larissa Ione

"Carrie Ann Ryan writes sexy shifters in a world full of passionate happily-ever-afters." – *New York Times* Bestselling Author Vivian Arend

"Carrie Ann's books are sexy with characters you can't help but love from page one. They are heat and heart blended to perfection." *New York Times* Bestselling Author Jayne Rylon

Carrie Ann Ryan's books are wickedly funny and deliciously hot, with plenty of twists to keep you guessing. They'll keep you up all night!" USA Today Bestselling Author Cari Quinn

"Once again, Carrie Ann Ryan knocks the Dante's Circle series out of the park. The queen of hot, sexy, enthralling paranormal romance, Carrie Ann is an author not to miss!" *New York Times* bestselling Author Marie Harte

MATED IN DARKNESS

As Tracker for the Redwood Pack, Kaylee Jamenson knows her duty. She's seen war and heartache, but now the battle hits closer to home when a Packmate goes missing. With rogues on the rise, the Alphas of the Redwood and Talon Packs send her to find their lost wolf before all is lost.

Yet nothing is as it seems and as the hunt grows dangerous, so does the threat to her heart when fate throws a curveball in her path.

Her mate.

# CHAPTER 1

Kaylee

THE WOLF in front of me snarled and I glared at the stranger with red fur before I slid to the side, their claws raking down my skin. I cursed under my breath, rolled in the dirt, and shook off the pain.

Another wolf came at me, its dark fur sleek under the fading light, and pushed me to the ground before he jumped at the wolf who had clawed me.

I sighed, rolled my eyes, and got back up. "Conner, stop it."

My twin didn't pay me any attention, but I didn't think he would.

This was why Conner and I were rarely on patrol together. The twin bond was a *thing*, and a growly overprotective twin brother who thought because he was a fraction more dominant than his baby sister that she needed protecting meant that the two of us should not be fighting together.

However, we were just out for a stroll, the two of us taking time between our shifts because we enjoyed each other's presence.

It wasn't our fault that the rogue had come at us—a rogue that we hadn't even realized was out in the woods outside the Redwood Pack den.

My brother needed to remember that I was a dominant wolf, and I knew what I was doing. I was an enforcer for my cousin, Gina. She expected me to be able to fight, and I did. Conner was also an enforcer, and that meant he thought he needed to protect me at all times. No matter that I was bleeding, in quite a bit of pain, and my wolf kept batting at me.

Conner had shifted quickly, the ability coming to him faster than most of our generation. I didn't have that kind of time, and so I had stayed in my human form.

Most wolves took at least a few minutes, if not longer, to shift into our wolf forms, but Conner could do it almost instantly if he needed to.

He'd be shit later, and he'd sleep hard and eat his

weight in carbs and protein, but he could shift in a blink of an eye.

He'd seen the rogue come at us and shifted after stripping down quickly. He'd become his wolf at the exact moment I let my claws out to fight the wolf who'd lost his humanity and wanted to end our lives.

The Redwoods had been through more than one war to protect our people, as well as every single human, witch, and shifter on Earth.

I had been part of two of those wars, one against the humans when they had realized those things that went bump in the night were real.

The other against the Aspens when their former Alpha had tried to take down the Talons. The Talons were our allies, so much so we were practically one Pack at this point.

When they'd needed us, we'd fought alongside them. There had been losses, but we had done what we could to protect our people.

I pushed thoughts of the past from my mind and focused on the battle in front of me. The wolf seemed to be a lone wolf from the look of it, one who had gotten too close to their animal side and couldn't find their way out. I could handle this on my own, yet Conner kept standing in my way.

We were usually a better team than this, but Conner

was dealing with things in his own life that kept getting in the way of thinking—hence why he kept trying to save his poor little twin sister.

I snarled at my twin, knowing if I didn't get my head in the game and protect his flank, both of us would be dead.

If Conner wasn't going to let me fight completely, I would let him take the majority of it so he didn't get hurt, and then I would kick my twin's ass later.

If I didn't kick his ass, one of our parents would. If they knew what Conner was doing now, they wouldn't let him get away with it. Neither would any of our five siblings. Conner was the eldest, and right now, he was the jerk.

Conner let out a strained whine when the rogue bit at his flank and my claws went out, my fangs elongated, and I roared.

The ground shook beneath us at the sound and the rogue's head twisted towards me.

*That's right, little wolf. I'm more dominant than you. More dominant than many of the wolves in our Pack.*

I might be small, but I was mighty—at least according to my mother. That I was also in my thirties and I used that phrase didn't matter.

This wolf had hurt my brother, and now, if we couldn't control it, we're going to have to end its life.

That was the last thing we wanted, but the problem with this rogue was that its animal was too close to the surface, making it stronger and far more dangerous. That's why it took enforcers and the strongest of the most dominant wolves in the Pack to take them down.

I leaped, taking the wolf to the ground in a quick movement. It let out a shocked gasp and groaned again, its entire body shaking. I cursed under my breath and held my arm around its neck as it twisted and turned.

Bone snapped, tendons tore, and the wolf let out another pained moan.

Relief slid through me for an instant, because this wolf was shifting back.

If they could shift back, that meant maybe we didn't have to kill him.

The problem with rogues was that they killed indiscriminately, harming anyone in their path.

We were the protectors of this place, of the weaker shifters, of the witches, of the humans.

If we didn't take care of the wolves, others could get hurt, and it could ruin the tableau that our peace was at the moment.

The wolf finally finished shifting as I held it down, and I found myself holding a naked man, covered in blood, and crying into his hands.

He finally passed out, and I looked up at Conner,

who had changed back to human, and thankfully put on clothes. We were shifters and usually didn't care about nudity, but he was my twin brother. There were things I didn't need to see on a daily basis.

"We'll get them back to the den."

I nodded. "Did you call Dad?"

"Yeah, Dad's on his way."

Dad being Josh, while Reed was our Father.

We were the children of the Redwood Pack Triad, the legendary story of Reed's, Hannah's, and Josh's romance bringing thrills to anyone who heard it.

There was even a movie coming out about their romance. As one intrepid reporter had heard about it through the grapevine and had written the story on their own, some of it was embellished, at least according to my mother, but most of it seemed a little too genuine.

Not that I needed to see the graphic scenes that were going to be the triad that are my parents.

I shook my head and pushed those thoughts from my mind.

"This is the fourth rogue this month," I whispered, and Conner nodded, his jaw tightening.

After we had found peace with the Aspens, we had a little bit of time to breathe, but not enough.

The Aspen Pack was dealing with their new hierarchy and were being quiet. The Talons were the ones that dealt with them more often than we did, because they were closer in proximity and in connections. Though I was an enforcer for my cousin, I wasn't in the hierarchy where it came to being 'in the know' for some things.

The little bit of peace hadn't been enough for those that were too close to their animals. Rogues were all around the nation, and they were starting to attract news stories.

That was a problem because we shifters were out in the open now, and though our current president was a fan of shifters and had them in the family, he would be up for re-election soon, and laws could be changed.

We needed to act like the civilized shifters that we were to keep the peace that we so desperately craved.

If we weren't careful, whatever was driving these rogues, if it were something beyond the Moon Goddess, would be trouble.

Thankfully, our wolves now had the Supreme Alphas, a mated pair in the Talons that I knew decently well, who were taking charge of it and making sure that the world knew that we were on top of things.

Our cousin, Parker, the Voice of the Wolves, was also in the thick of things. He was the shining face and beacon for all those who wanted to see a wolf in action with a smile. He was the one who connected the Packs across the world, as it was his role placed on him by the Moon Goddess.

He was also the one that was getting on my last nerve because he needed my power. He wanted me to use it more than I was, but since I still didn't have complete control over it, that wasn't easy.

Not out of hatred or selfishness, but because my power was special.

I could find anyone in the world once I got their scent, their sight, or a vision. My dad, Josh, was the same way, though he was human.

Out of all of us seven siblings, we'd each received something special from our parents.

As Reed was a wolf of immense power with beautiful talents in art, some of my siblings took a shine to him. Our mother, Hannah, was a powerful earth witch, possibly the most powerful earth witch in the country, and a couple of my siblings held an affinity for her magic as well.

I was the only one with Dad's genes that held through.

That meant I would have to leave the den soon to help find a certain rogue, and one of our Packmates that had gone after him.

A Packmate we hadn't heard from in far too long.

I felt the itch between my shoulder blades. I knew I would have to leave soon.

Only, something told me I wasn't ready. Or maybe that was me telling myself I couldn't be prepared.

Conner helped me subdue the man and ensure he wouldn't wake up soon and hurt someone, and we covered him with my jacket.

I looked up into the tree line as Parker walked through, a couple of our fellow enforcers with him.

"Another one," Parker whispered, his wolf in his gaze as the gold rim around his irises glowed.

I cringed. "Another one."

"We're running out of time, Kaylee."

"Stop ordering her around," Conner growled.

I rolled my eyes. "I can take care of myself, numbnuts."

"Love the attitude, sister of mine," he mumbled, and I let go of the rogue as the other enforcers took him from me.

Parker helped me up, frowning. "Come on. Kade wants to meet with us."

My wolf stood at attention, keening for their Alpha.

Kade was my uncle, our Alpha, and a man that I truly loved. I loved our huge family, the way that we took care of one another, and were always there for each other no matter what.

I did not want to leave the den.

Only, I knew I was running out of time, and so were the rogues taking over the country.

Parker needed me to find our Packmate, to ensure that they weren't one of the rogues out there. I knew that once I met with Kade, I would be under an Alpha's orders, and there would be no going back.

I killed two rogues this month alone, and nearly had to kill a third. If the man unconscious in the truck in front of me didn't wake sane, our Pack would have to kill him too.

A darkness was coming. I could feel it in my bones.

My Pack had been through hell and back, and all I wanted was peace, only I didn't think it was coming.

My wolf was antsy, tired of staying here, needing to be free, needing to find a resolution that I was afraid would never come.

So I stood on the precipice of two choices, both paths I wasn't ready to take.

Yet, I knew one would be laid before me, and I wouldn't have a choice. I was the Tracker of the Redwood Pack, and it was my turn to protect those I loved.

No matter the cost.

# CHAPTER 2

Kaylee

I STOOD in front of my Alpha, my Uncle Kade, who was shaking his head. My wolf bowed, my gaze not directly meeting Kade's. It wasn't out of anger or fear. It was because, while I was a dominant wolf, Kade's dominance was out of this world. It was why he was Alpha, and I didn't even have a title within the Pack hierarchy. Oh yes, I was a dominant, and I was an enforcer, but I wasn't *the* Enforcer. I wasn't the Beta, or Heir, or Healer. Those went to my other cousins, the ones the Moon Goddess had blessed with their powers.

I was a Tracker, though, and while most Packs had

more than one Tracker, my place had been given to me not because of the Moon Goddess, but because of my genetic disposition. While I understood that, it was always odd not to be the blessed one from the Moon Goddess herself.

"We can't find Spencer. It's been nearly a week since we've heard from him," Kade growled, and the others in the room nodded along. "We need to search for him, though, because something's wrong. I can still feel his connection to the Pack, so he's alive, but he's not returning to us. That means something has him. I'm afraid he'll go rogue if he's out of touch for too long."

I stood between Conner and Parker and nodded along, worry in my gut over our Packmate.

Spencer had lost the woman who should have been his mate during the battles. They hadn't completed the bond, and therefore he hadn't had the full blowback of magic from losing a mate, but he had lost the *potential*.

It was a horrible feeling that stretched within one's soul and scratched beneath the surface for eons, a feeling I never wanted to even think about.

He had been close to going rogue since, though our family and Pack had done our best to keep Spencer sane. To help him feel as if he had a reason for being.

I thought it'd been working. Our Healer, Mark, had been doing his best to help, and the Omega, Drake, was healing any emotional wounds he could. However, it was hard for both of them to do their job when Spencer kept pulling away.

He had gone on a trip for his work in the human world and he hadn't returned. His boss had said that he had up and quit, leaving them hanging, and it worried all of us.

Only, for now, Spencer didn't feel like a rogue with the Pack bonds, and that's what confused all of us.

"I'm going to send out two of my Trackers, though on separate paths," Kade began.

Gina nodded. "Yes, Nick will go out east, to where he was supposed to have his business meeting, but Kaylee? You're going to use your power to find him."

"I'll do my best," I said, the Pack bonds tugging on me. My power as a Tracker didn't work the same way as my dad's did. Nor did it work like any other Tracker. It was off and on and had more to do with my wolf's mood than it did me.

"You'll need to meet with the Packs where you go, as you're going to be on their territory," Parker explained. He was the Voice of the Wolves, the one that had slowly allowed us to all come together in the new century rather than fighting amongst ourselves. At least he had gotten us on the right path. Parker, although he was my cousin, was no longer even a Redwood. He had mated into a triad of his own with the Talons. As one of his mates was part of the hierarchy, it had made sense for his wolf to choose to go to the Talons. And yet, part of me could still feel him along the Redwood bonds, as if our two Packs were truly becoming one conglomerate over time.

I knew some of the wolves in both Packs were uneasy about it, as change always brought new circumstances we weren't always ready for, but if it meant that my family could be with me, those that went to the Talons and those that stayed, I was happy.

"When do you want me to leave?" I asked, ignoring Conner's warning growl beside me.

Kade glared at Conner, and my twin shut right up. My brother did not want me to have anything to do with what was going to happen, and while I understood that, he would have to deal.

"Tomorrow morning's fine. We can get you out on a flight there. One of our own will fly you on our plane."

I grinned at that, as did Kade. We had always had small planes to get us where we were going, but now that we were out in the open, we didn't have to hide exactly who we were and where we got our money.

That meant we had our own private airfield for the Packs and could fly without dealing with identification issues.

After all, some of my family members were well into their three-hundreds. As shifters lived very long lives, having to constantly change their identification for the humans got a little cumbersome. We could use our passports that said the age that we wanted them to know, or we could fly on our own airline.

The world was changing, but we were making do.

"Are you going alone?" Conner asked.

Our Alpha sighed. "She's a Tracker, a dominant wolf, and my niece. I wouldn't send her out alone if she couldn't handle it. You're needed here, Conner. You know why."

My twin lowered his head, submitting to his Alpha, and to his uncle's chiding. I knew why Conner needed to stay. He just didn't want to.

Though we were in a time of peace, the rogues meant that that peace might break soon. Tension was on the horizon, and that meant all of us needed to be at our best. Conner needed to stop fighting with everybody around him.

I got my orders, I knew when I needed to fly out, but instead of heading to my small home on the other side of the den, I headed to the first home that I'd had within these walls.

My parents were inside, the smell of hearth and home and their three scents wrapped around me. My mother hugged me tight and she kissed the top of my head, her dark curly hair a little wild as she had been outside working.

"I hear you're going on a trip," Mom said as she led me in.

"Do you need me to go with you?" Dad asked, and I shot Conner a look.

My twin held up both hands. "I didn't ask. It has nothing to do with me."

"No, that would just be Josh being overprotective," Reed said as he kissed his husband's temple. "You do know that Josh is a Tracker, though, so he can go with you if you need him."

My wolf bristled, but my father's wolf was more dominant than mine, so it wasn't like I could push back too much.

"I'm fine. If I need help, I will call you. All of you. I can take rogues down on my own, and we know that going into another Pack's territory means it is better to go one at a time. Especially because we don't know the Starlight Pack that well."

The Starlight Pack was in southern Texas, the starting point for my search. I wasn't sure why I knew that, but it just clung to me, part of my tracking. After all, Spencer was from down there. Maybe he had gone home. Or maybe my wolf was twisting me up into knots because I couldn't tell.

It wasn't like I could imagine a golden thread to lead me down there. It was just my wolf pushing me in that direction. But I could be wrong and following the wrong path.

"Where is Nick going?"

"Out to Philadelphia," Conner said as he hugged Mom. "That's where he should have been for his business meeting."

"But if you feel that you need to go down to the Starlight Pack, that's where he probably is," my mom said softly.

"Not necessarily. My tracking isn't as good as Dad's. I'm going to find him. Even if I have to go back up to Philly."

"We'll see," Dad said, frowning.

"You know my tracking is hit or miss unless I have an emotional connection to my target these days."

He nodded, but before I could say anything else, my other siblings walked in.

Nico, Addison, Monica, Redmond, and Brodie all tumbled in, laughing and acting like adolescents rather than the twenty-somethings they all were.

My parents went big or went home, and I couldn't help but laugh.

Some of us looked more like Reed than Josh, so we knew who our genetic father was, but both men had raised us, along with our mom. How my mom had gone through labor and delivery so many times, I didn't know, but I knew that on Mother's Day she always got the best flowers and a day off. After all, she'd had to help raise us. We were little terrors.

"No more talk of tracking before dinner," my mom said as she nodded tightly. "We are going to have a good dinner and not have a food fight, as you guys aren't five anymore, and then we're going to go to the Pack circle and listen to the Moon Goddess."

My brows rose. "When is the last time that we did that?" I asked, looking at my sisters.

Both Addison and Monica just shrugged.

"I just feel like we need to do it," Mom said. "I know it's weird, but we're going to go down and stand in the circle as a family. We don't need to offer a sacrifice or build an altar, that's not what we do, but I feel like we need to respect the Moon Goddess."

"Doesn't she speak directly to Cheyenne and Max now?" Conner asked.

"As they're the Supreme Alphas, that is true," Reed said as he helped the others set the table. "It's not like we can just ask our friends to go draw up a line. And they're not here anyway."

I blinked. "Where are they?"

"They're in DC meeting with the President of the United States. Big things. Then they're off to the Thames Pack to go meet with that Alpha, Allister."

I grinned. "How is the Alpha?" I practically purred, and Addison cackled.

"Too old for you," Josh growled, sounding much more like a shifter than a human.

"Didn't you go on a date with him?" Monica asked softly.

"We had coffee, and he was nice, but I'm never going to go out on a *date* date with the man. I'm not going to mate with the Alpha of the Thames Pack. I would never get used to driving on the wrong side of the road."

Mom winked. "If he were your mate, we would be happy for you, even though we would miss you. Technology is great, and we can see each other often these days, but I don't even like you living outside of the house, let alone so far away."

"The Alpha of the Pack in England is not my mate," I said drily.

"But he is dreamy," Monica sighed, and the rest of our brothers groaned.

"You would think we were all teenagers and not full adults all in the process of mating on our own. I mean, our cousins have children. Maybe it's time we find our mates."

"I was far older than you by the time I found your dad and mom," Father said. "In fact, all of my siblings, other than Cailin, were either near one hundred or over it by the time that we found our mates."

"I don't want to wait that long," Monica sighed.

"Same here," Nico put in.

"Well, I'm not going to be tracking for a mate. I'm going to be tracking for a part of our Pack. So I should probably focus on that, and not on a certain swoony Alpha." My wolf pushed at me, and I knew she was anxious to find our forever. Only, I didn't know when that would happen. I couldn't put out an ad for a mate, so I'd have to wait.

My twin just rolled his eyes, and my mom tapped me on the nose. "Only happy talk. We'll talk of the serious soon."

I grinned, kissed my mother on the cheek, and stole a roll.

"Okay then, talk of the happy, and then we talk of magic."

Because we were family, we were Pack, and we were Redwoods.

# CHAPTER 3

Kaylee

IF MY TWIN didn't stop glaring at me, I'd have to slash him with my claws and prove who could be more dominant. Conner might be slightly more dominant than me most days, but thanks to the twin bond, I could take his wolf if a strong emotion took over me. With my twin wanting to coddle me like usual, that emotion wouldn't be hard to find.

We were at the same place in the hierarchy, with our individual talents leading us to similar paths, but he still treated me like the baby sister, and I resented it. It didn't matter that we had five other siblings. I was the first baby to him.

I wanted to nip at him just because.

"Stop growling at your brother," Mom whispered from my side, and I leaned into her, scowling down at her. She was a few inches shorter than me, even though I wasn't too tall, but Mom was a compact powerhouse.

"He's glaring at me. What do you expect?"

"Reed is telling him to stop. We're here to find peace as a family before you go off on your journey. It's hard to watch your children grow and make choices and take chances that could hurt them. Even though at the same time it's fulfilling and wonderful that your babies are well rounded and nurtured enough to be enforcers for the Pack."

I smiled and kissed the top of her head. "You're the best, Mom. All of your chicks are leaving the nest and finding their places."

"I have no idea how it happened. At least I don't look a day over thirty. If we weren't part of the Pack with magic that leads to longevity, I know all of you would have turned me gray after your first birthdays."

I laughed, shaking my head. "We try our best." I sighed and looked out at the Pack circle, where we had come for the evening. We weren't there for a ceremony or a true event, but coming here as a family had always brought us a sense of peace. We would stand in the circle, link hands, and allow our family's magic to run through our familial bonds.

I wasn't sure if our cousins or other Packmates ever did this, but it was our thing nonetheless. I'd never heard the Moon Goddess speak to me while we did it, I didn't think any of us had, but it brought us closer together.

"Ready to go?" Brodie asked as he bounced over. He kissed my temple and took my hand, leading me to the center of the circle.

The Pack circle had been a place of bloodshed, heartache, and monumental decisions in the past, and I knew it would one day be so again, and soon. The stone stadium had been carved into the side of the mountain, the center area packed dirt from centuries of wolves settling their paths over time.

This was where dominance challenges, Pack meetings, and other important events were held, and was where I had become an enforcer of the Pack. Kade had cemented a new layer on the bond that connected me to him and the others, and my wolf had preened. I'd stood next to my brother, and the two of us had been welcomed into our new prospective roles in the Pack, alongside a few of my cousins, and I'd never been prouder to be a Jamenson.

Now we were here as a smaller part of our immense

family, knowing I would be off on my journey within the hour. Spencer needed me, and my wolf clawed at me to find him.

"Ready?" Josh asked, a small smile on his face even though I saw the worry in his gaze.

Josh, Reed, and Hannah had fought demons, wolves, and the end of the world to save their family and each other. It was a lot to live up to, and I had to pray to the Moon Goddess I'd find a way.

"Ready," I whispered.

Then I held Brodie's hand, took my mother's free one, and closed my eyes. We didn't speak. We didn't need to. We just let the power flow through us, protection, warmth, and love gliding over us as if this had been what we'd been searching for all of our lives.

Having a witch, a human, and a wolf as our parents set us apart from the others ever so slightly, and we used that for our gain. The Pack needed us, and we needed the Pack.

Pack was family.

Pack was one.

We were Pack.

WHEN WE WERE DONE WE CAMPED OUT IN THE center for a snack, because it was hard to leave and we liked being with one another. Addison, Monica, Redmond, and Brodie were off to the side, going over plans for the week in their roles for the Pack. Nico stood with our parents, frowning at something Dad was saying, and I wanted to ask what it was, but I needed to focus on what my wolf was nudging me toward.

Spencer needed me, and I needed to focus on finding him.

Conner and I were off to the side near the trees, my wolf unnerved and anxious, and my twin rarely let me out of his sight when his wolf was on edge. I didn't blame him, even if I wanted to.

"I don't want you to go."

I narrowed my eyes. "Why? Because you think I can't handle it? Or because you want to go and prove yourself? You know I'm a Tracker. This is my *job*. You have other responsibilities here."

He ran his hands through his hair in a quick and jerky motion. "Of course I believe in you, Kaylee. That's not the problem. I don't want to be a Tracker. That's your thing."

"Then what is it?"

"I have a bad feeling, okay? I don't know what it is, but I feel like if you go, something bad will happen, and I'm not going to be there to protect you. And I know you hate that, but we protect *each other*. I won't be there, and you could get hurt." He rubbed a fist over his chest. "You *will* get hurt. I can feel it."

I froze, my wolf at attention. "You don't get visions, Conner. It's just a bad feeling. It's not a prophecy."

I didn't know if I was telling myself or him. I'd never seen him this way, and it scared me. We were closer to each other than we were to our other siblings, closer than we were to anyone else. And though he annoyed me to no end, he was my brother, my twin. Since he was this worried, I wanted to tell him that I would stay and figure something else out, but we both knew that couldn't happen. I had a job. A duty. Same as him. Spencer needed me to find him, needed me to follow the trial of evidence and hope to the Moon Goddess that my Tracker ability would kick in and the sense of knowing would intensify.

I couldn't stay to alleviate my twin's worry, and it killed me.

"I'm not the Foreseer of the Pack. I *know* that. It's just...I don't know, Kaylee. I'm worried, and I've never been this worried before. I don't know what the hell I'm going to do if you get hurt, sister mine. My wolf is so close to the surface these days. We both know that. What if you get hurt and I go rogue?"

And there it was, the stark honesty of his words and the pain slicing between us both over the twin bond.

With the new powers in the supernatural world, rogues were intensifying, we all knew it, but we didn't know what we were going to do about it. We could do our best to stop them once they turned, to find a way for them to go find a new normal and reality, but we couldn't prevent them. Not when we didn't know the root of the problem.

Conner was nowhere near going rogue, but I knew my words wouldn't be able to help him, not when he was this worried. If we weren't careful, not even our Alpha and Omega would be able to keep him from turning into a self-fulfilling prophecy.

I stepped forward and hugged him, wrapping my arms around his middle and holding tight. "I love you, Conner. I'm going to be okay, and even if something happens to me while I'm there, you won't go rogue. My wolf won't allow it." I growled those last words, the twin bond between us flaring.

"That doesn't instill me with confidence, Kaylee." He snarled the words, but he still hugged me back.

"I don't know what else I'm supposed to say, other than we've both trained for this, and this is my duty. I have to trust my skills and the Pack I'm visiting to ensure I don't fall down a hole and get lost or something."

He snorted, exactly as I wanted him to, before he squeezed me tightly once more and stepped back. He shook himself, his eyes gold with his wolf. Yes, Conner had always been closer to his wolf than most of us, but it wasn't a problem. There were others who were even more tightly wound with their wolves and rarely let the gold seep away. We all had different relationships with the souls that resided around ours, and I knew from the bottom of my heart that Conner would be okay. His wolf protected him just as he protected those around him.

He had to find the faith to believe in that, to believe that I would be fine.

And though I wanted to say something more, I couldn't, not when I was worried. I was going into an unusual situation, to a place I'd never been, and while I would have liked backup, we didn't have that kind of relationship with the Starlight Pack.

I'd find my way and hopefully, if the Moon Goddess could help us, find Spencer.

Because if we didn't, if we lost another Packmate, I wasn't sure what Conner would do, or the other enforcers for that matter. The rogues were increasing, and if we weren't careful, our Pack could be the one that produced the next set of rogues.

Killing another friend would destroy me.

Killing my brother would end me.

# CHAPTER 4

Kaylee

I WASN'T a fan of flying, though it had nothing to do with heights. My wolf needed to be free and have the choice to roam, and flying didn't give us that option. I wanted to pace up and down the aisle so I could at least move, but I didn't want to tip off the attendant and pilots in the small private plane that the Pack owned that I wasn't comfortable with flying.

By the time we landed, I was on edge and wanted to run in my fur, but I couldn't yet. First, I needed to meet with the Alpha of the Starlight Pack and ensure he knew I wasn't there to poach on his territory. I might be a Tracker, but I had rules to follow, and I didn't need his people to think I was a rogue trying to take over their Pack.

The Starlight Pack was a large Pack in south Texas, outside of San Antonio. Their territory went east and held some of the coastal areas on the gulf as well. While I knew Kade was more dominant than Riaz—their Alpha—it was only by just a little. They were a strong Pack, and I understood that, thanks to my cousin Parker, we were working on forming an alliance. It was slow going, and I knew we were working with other partners as well. I knew it was for the best.

After centuries of our Packs becoming so insular some had folded inward, we were becoming a power and coming into the new century. We needed to strengthen our bonds with one another because something was coming. We weren't sure what. Even the Foreseers couldn't see beneath the veil of shadow around us.

I stepped off the plane into the suffocating heat and wanted to pant like my wolf. It was a humid heat that made my hair begin to stand up off my shoulders, and I held in a growl. I might be used to humidity, thanks to living in the Pacific Northwest, but I wasn't used to it attached to heat.

"Kaylee Jamenson?" a deep voice asked from beside me, and I turned toward the man. I'd scented him the moment the plane door opened, my wolf on alert for the predator in our midst.

The man in front of me had a wide build, thick muscle roping his body, and dark hair. He looked as if he spent a lot of time outdoors, his skin a deep tan, and his hazel eyes sliced anyone he glared at. Though he scented of dominant wolf, he didn't have the ring of gold around his eyes, telling me he had complete control of the shifter within.

He met my gaze, and I his, not blinking or turning away. I might not be in my own Pack, or even near anyone I knew, but I wasn't going to submit to anyone just because I was a stranger and a woman who happened to be of average size. I wasn't as petite as some of my family members, but I wasn't the tallest either.

It took nearly a full minute, but finally the other man turned away, seeming to look behind me in order to save face. I let him, as he'd been the one to begin the dominance battle and hadn't once growled or shown his wolf to me. It seemed to be reflex to him, and I wasn't in the mood to see who's was bigger this early in the search.

As it was, the connection that pulsated between the Pack and me, those bonds that weren't always visible since I wasn't an Alpha or in the highest hierarchies, pulled at me, and I let out a breath.

"That's me. And you are?"

"Brendan. I'm Beta here to the Starlight Pack. Welcome to our home. You alone?"

I nodded, looking past him when he faced me again. "I am. Just like promised. I'm here to see if I sense Spencer. Have you heard from him?"

Brendan shook his head, his shoulders stiffening. "No, we haven't. Not even his parents, which is worrisome. When he joined the Redwoods after going lone wolf a couple of decades ago, it surprised us, since he usually liked staying to himself, but he sounded happy."

My heart clenched and I nodded. "I don't know him well, but yes, he is happy. He has friends but lost the woman that would have been his mate during the battles."

Brendan cursed. "I didn't know that."

It ached to even think about, but I ignored the pain. "We haven't heard from him in over a week, though he should have been back from his trip out east a few days ago. We have another Packmate looking from him there with another Pack. I'm here to track him with what we have and hope we can find him."

"You're a Tracker then."

I nodded. "Not in the sense like a full Tracker would be, but I have the skills." A full Tracker was blessed by the Moon Goddess with the title. My skills came from my DNA, thanks to Josh. While the Beta looked curious, I didn't elaborate. I wasn't about to lie to him about who I was, but he didn't need to know every single part of where I had come from and what our powers were. We weren't allies yet.

"We'll help where we can. You'll have whatever you need. First, though, you need to meet with Riaz."

I nodded. "Of course." I couldn't enter their lands without meeting the Alpha and being welcomed into the Pack as a guest. If other members of the Pack found me roaming on their lands in search for Spencer without the Alpha's welcome, it could be a declaration of war. While it might not make sense to humans, it had helped our Packs stay safe for centuries—even with new technology and the fact that our existence was now out to the humans.

We had rules to keep us alive.

And if we didn't follow them, our lives were rightly forfeit.

I nodded at Brendan and followed him to the car nearby. I focused on my wolf, trying to see if it was telling me anything, and the other wolf frowned at me.

"Did you find anything yet?" he asked as he started the engine. I shook my head. "It takes me a minute to get through the discombobulation of changing settings, if that makes sense."

"If your power's attached to your Pack and your

location, that makes sense. You're not near your Pack, not near where you grew up, not near anything that you know. It's going to take you a minute to find that pulse."

I gave the other wolf a look and raised a brow. "Intuitive."

"We don't have trackers like you in this Pack, but we're all wolves with bonds to the Moon Goddess. We learned a few things over time."

I nodded and focused inward, trying to catch any movement inside that would be lead me to Spencer.

"I remember Spencer when he was younger and living here," the other man said after a moment.

I looked up at him. "Oh?"

"He's a good man. Or at least he was when I knew him. He calls his parents every week, even now, after so many years. Even when he was a lone wolf, he would make sure his parents knew that he was safe and unharmed. During your war with the Centrals? He made sure that his family knew he was safe. And then again, when the humans attacked us? He was there."

"Did the government come for your Pack too?" I asked, aware I didn't know the history of this Pack.

The other man scowled. "They tried. We were one of the Packs that weren't living out in the open, but it's not like we can hide in a forest like some of you guys."

I scowled. "Because you don't have forests?"

He snorted. "We were on hill country, but it's a little different than an actual Redwood forest."

"True." I paused. "They came after you then?"

He nodded as he pulled up onto a dirt road, and I could sense other wolves nearby. We must be nearing the center of their den, or at least the part they would allow me to see.

"They did. We didn't let them get far. They didn't come in as hard as they did with you, as they didn't know much about us, but like they were doing with much of the wolves around the country, they were trying to set a precedent, give us a message. They weren't able to."

"I'm glad that you were able to protect yourself."

"The Starlight Pack is stronger than most people think."

"I knew you were strong. Why do you think I came alone and didn't try to make my way in with another enforcer?"

"Because it would have been a sign of aggression. Maybe one day our Packs will be friendly enough that it won't be an issue. But not now."

"Maybe one day."

"I mean, not all of us can inter-mate with another Pack so much that you and the Talons seem like you're kissing cousins at this point."

I scowled. "Really? That's what you're going with?"

"Just saying." He let a small smile escape before scowling again as he pulled in.

"This won't take long. You meet with Riaz, and then we'll help you find your Packmate. Our Packmate."

My wolf bristled. "He's not Starlight anymore. He hasn't been for a while."

"He's family. You understand that."

"I do. Let's go find him."

"But first, Riaz."

Meeting a new Alpha wasn't my favorite thing to do. Going through the dominance games with Brendan had been enough for the day, and I was going to have to deal with it again meeting the Alpha of the Starlight Pack.

I didn't have time for this, and I couldn't feel the pull towards Spencer, and that worried me.

I held onto whatever feeling I could and rolled my shoulders back, aware that others were watching me, but it didn't feel hostile. More like curious.

I figured that was a good thing, and I made my way through, not meeting anyone's gaze, mostly because I didn't want to have to deal with the dominance challenge. We wouldn't be able to help ourselves. We were wolves. It was in our nature.

We made our way around to a new development within the den, and I realized that no, we weren't actually in the den itself. I hadn't gone through any wards. We were on the outside of the den still, and I understood that. They didn't want me within their den walls, at least not before I met the Alpha, and I was grateful that they had that kind of security. But they were building something outside of it, which was interesting. I looked at the shirtless man in front of me as he helped put up the side of a building, the others around him equally shirtless in the Texas heat, as they worked on the framing of what looked to be a small home.

The man with dark eyes and dark hair looked at me and raised a brow. "Kaylee then?" the man asked.

I didn't meet his gaze. He was the Alpha, and he was far more dominant than me. I could feel it, but he also didn't growl or show his wolf. He just set his tools down and picked up a towel to wipe the sweat off his body.

He was hot as hell, built, and any woman's dream, but my wolf wanted nothing to do with him.

And considering my wolf wanted a mate and didn't want to just scratch an itch, I listened to my wolf.

He was an attractive Alpha with strength in numbers and a cunning intelligence, from what I had heard, and my wolf didn't want him.

Well, that would make my mother happy because she didn't want me to move down away from her.

"Alpha Riaz."

"Well met. Thank you for coming here to help find your lost Packmate, one of ours. You have our resources, anything that you need. If you need to stay for more than a few nights, we have guest quarters outside of the den. They're guarded by our lieutenants, as well as other dominant wolves. You will be housed, fed, anything that you need. You name it."

I looked at his face, my gaze slightly below his. "That's generous of you. Thank you."

"Thank you for coming here to help find Spencer. We've been looking, but we can't catch his scent." His jaw tightened. "I'm afraid it's because he's turned rogue," he said, and you could've heard a pin drop.

I swallowed hard and nodded. "That's my fear too. Although he was a lone wolf for a long time; I don't picture him ever going rogue, and that's what worries me."

"It worries us too. I have a call coming in with your Alpha and Gideon, the Alpha of the Talon Pack, to discuss the rogue situation. We're having similar interactions with rogues as you are up there."

"You might want to loop in the Alphas of the Centrals and the Aspens," I added.

Riaz raised a brow. "I was unaware that you had full allyship with them."

"Those two Alphas are newer in power than you or any of the Alphas that I answer to, but they still have knowledge."

I wasn't about to discuss the law and history of the Aspens and the Centrals with us, but most people knew a lot of it anyway.

"I'll reach out to them."

"Kade would reach out to them nonetheless, but it would show goodwill for you to do so."

"You sounded like your cousin just then," Riaz said, a smirk on his face.

This time I rolled my eyes, the tension leaking out of me. "Parker is training me to be diplomatic. I'm better than my twin, but not the greatest."

"Good to know. Do you want to begin, or do you want to rest after traveling?"

My wolf stood on attention, and I rolled my shoulders back. "I need to begin. I think I have something."

And with that, the hunt began.

# CHAPTER 5

Kaylee

MY WOLF CLAWED AT ME, wanting out, but I wasn't about to shift and make myself vulnerable in front of people I didn't know. I would have to soon if I wanted to get the scent later, but for now, I let my wolf rise to the surface, so my eyes were glowing gold and lighting up the area around me, but I was still in control.

The two wolves from the Starlight Pack behind me were lieutenants for the Pack enforcer. They weren't anyone I had met on the airfield or even in the Pack circle with their Alpha. However, they were dominant, intelligent, and had a purpose. They wanted to find Spencer as much as I did.

Maybe more because both of them had said they had been childhood friends of the man.

My heart twisted at the thought, the idea that Spencer had left his Pack behind because his wolf had needed to roam, and when he had settled in the Redwood den, Spencer had begun to create roots, paths, and connections.

He wasn't a wolf that was supposed to go rogue, but then the war with the humans, and then the Aspens, have created battle and war after war, and Spencer had lost the woman that was supposed to be his mate.

They hadn't forged a bond but had instead taken their time doing their own courting.

Not all wolves mated the same, and thanks to the Moon Goddess's intervention a few years ago, things were dramatically different than they had been even when my parents had mated.

Now, there was more of a choice in the matter, and it took longer for others to find their mate. As if there was a cloud or a shadow over the bond that could be created between two or more souls.

It had taken my cousin years to figure out what the bond between them could be, and another cousin had mated at first sight.

It depended on the wolves, but I knew matings were harder to come by because of the fact that our connections to the Moon Goddess had changed. She had made a sacrifice for us, at least according to the Supreme Alphas. I wasn't sure what that was, nor did I know if they knew, but how wolves reacted with the rest of the world had changed.

Not to mention that everything that I had thought was true for my thirty-something years was wrong.

Wolves and witches weren't the only paranormals out there. Yes, there were demons, but those had been sent to their dimension, especially after Caym had tried to decimate our Pack, and they killed so many of us.

I tried not to think about him, though I had only been an infant when he had been taken out. I could still hear the pain and terror in my family's voice when they spoke of him.

However, there were more than the three major powers. The Aspen Pack had a cat shifter, and during a horrific turn of events that almost cost my friend's life, the Talon Pack also now had a cat shifter.

I knew there had to be many other secrets out there since the world so was much bigger than us. After all, I couldn't be the only Tracker like my father. There had to be more. Only my family had never been able to find out *why* Josh was that way or why I was the only one of their children to inherit his traits.

I pushed this outside of my mind and followed the scent and trail towards Spencer.

"Do you feel him?" Rio, one of the lieutenants, asked, and I nodded. "Slightly. It keeps fading in and out, so I don't know if he's moving farther away or my wolf continues to lose sight of him." I frowned. "I don't like the idea of that, though."

"Neither do I. We haven't been able to find Spencer since we thought that he could be out here," the other wolf, Dane, said.

I looked over at him and saw he had a frown on his face that only made the scar on his cheek more prominent.

"Our Alpha called you ahead then, to look?" I asked, trying to pick up on Spencer's scent. I couldn't at all, and that worried me. I just had to hope that my Tracking wasn't leading us astray.

My cousin was still in Philadelphia, searching for Spencer, but nobody had seen him for the conference he was supposed to be at. There was no scent, no place to track.

Either he was in the wrong place, or we both were, and we were never going to be able to find Spencer. I pushed those thoughts from my mind, not wanting to think about them.

"Yes, as did your Beta," Dane answered. "They told us when he hadn't shown up and thought maybe he would come out here. Now that you're here, it just reaffirms the fact that we need to find out."

"Because I'm the Tracker?" I asked, ducking underneath a fallen branch.

Rio picked it up as if it weighed nothing, and he looked down at me, interest in his gaze.

They were both dominant wolves, strong enough to match my own wolf, and yet I felt nothing.

My wolf wanted a mate. She didn't want just a quick lay to get rid of her aggression and need.

That meant I had to deal with it.

I gave him a small smile, then went back to Tracking, and I figured the way that I turned would be enough of an answer to the question in his gaze.

He didn't push, and I was grateful. I hated having to put down dominant wolves when I wasn't in the mood to deal with their games. I was a dominant wolf myself, I understood.

But I had to listen to my own needs. For once.

My phone buzzed, and I cursed and pulled it out of my pocket. "Sorry."

"No problem, we'll keep on the scent," Dane said, as he gestured towards Rio to move out of the way. We were werewolves, and so it was going to be hard for them to give me too much privacy, but they were at least giving me the benefit of the doubt.

That was nice considering I was an unknown on their territory.

"What is it, Conner?" I asked, my voice a growl.

"I'm just checking in on you. You don't have to snap at me." My brother grumbled into the phone, and I held back a smile. This wasn't a time to smile, not when something was sending me on edge.

"I'm Tracking right now, I don't have time for you to get possessive and growly."

"I just had a bad feeling along the twin bond. I don't know what it is. I feel like you're in the right place. It's just hard. You know?"

My wolf calmed slightly, liking to be reassured. I sighed. "I feel like we're in the right place too, and that worries me. Because I can't scent him, Conner. I don't know what we're going to find."

"If you don't want me out there, anyone else from the Pack can come fly out, so you're not alone. We're creating an alliance with the Starlight Pack. They won't mind."

"I'm not alone out here. There are two other lieutenants that are helpful."

"As long as they don't get in your way."

I held back a smile. "No, only you do that here." My wolf patted at me then, and I froze. "I've got to go. There's something. I think I scent something."

"Shit, Kaylee. Be careful."

"I will. I promise. There's just something out there."

"Don't be stupid."

"Thanks for that. I love you, too."

"I love you. Check-in."

"You know I will." I hung up the phone, stuck it back in my pocket, and trotted towards the lieutenants. "I have something."

"Okay. We're behind you." Dane pulled out his phone, and I gave him a look. "I'm texting our Alpha and giving him an update."

"Good. Let's go."

We moved through the trees, the live oaks tickling my nose. I hadn't realized I could have allergies as a wolf, but apparently the oaks and cedars down here were enough to make my eyes water. It was hard to scent through all of that, but I blew out through my nose and then sucked in another breath, trying to sense what I needed to, and my wolf froze, so still, I was afraid I saw death.

But that wasn't it, at least not yet.

"I scent him. He's close." I let out a low growl, my

claws sliding through my fingertips. "And he's not alone."

"On it," Rio said from my side.

We moved through the brush, quiet, stalking. We went in a three formation, having each other's backs while making sure we were silent enough.

I could scent Spencer now. We were so close. But that wasn't the only smell. Not even the stranger's scent could overpower the coppery scent that assaulted my nostrils.

Blood.

There was blood.

I moved through the trees, and the sight before me chilled the blood in my veins.

A man stood over Spencer's body, his hands over Spencer's chest, blood coating him. Spencer lay still, unmoving underneath the man's attentions, and I could already smell the rot and decay of newly made death.

A growl slipped through my lips, and I pounced, pulling the human back away from Spencer, and slammed the ryan into the soft muddy dirt. It didn't hurt him, it wouldn't break anything, but it was hard enough for him to let out an oof of air.

"Who are you?" I asked him, my voice a deep growl. I knew my fangs had elongated, my claws sharp enough to prick his skin. Even though my hand was around his neck, I was cautious not to make him bleed.

The man with green eyes and dark hair below me stiffened, and I ignored the sweet, honeyed scent of him that lay beneath the blood.

This man was human, not a witch, not a shifter. He held nothing but the knowledge of our existence like all the other humans in the world.

But he was covered in Spencer's blood, and I needed to know why.

"My name is Jason," the man growled, his voice deep, surprising me with the strength and tenacity.

"Why were you with Spencer? Why did you kill him?" I asked, because I knew the truth. Spencer was dead. Rio stood over Spencer's body, checking for a pulse, seeing if there was anything that we could do with a healer. Dane was behind me, protecting my flank, and I was grateful.

I didn't see a weapon on Jason, and if he wasn't a witch, that meant unless he had thrown the weapon away, Jason hadn't killed Spencer.

Somebody had, and I needed to know who.

And perhaps this Jason wasn't alone, and Dane would keep a watch out because first I needed to deal with the human below me.

"I found him like that. I've been searching for him."

I stilled, my wolf at attention. "Why?

"I'll explain everything. Can you please get your claws out of my skin?"

I tilted my head, a very wolf gesture. "You're not bleeding. You're just fine. You're going to tell me what you did to my wolf. Or you're not going to like what happens next."

Then the damned human did the strangest thing out of all. He smiled, even with the slight fear in his gaze, and my wolf pounced, knowing who she was seeing.

I cursed, loosened my grip ever so slightly, and growled.

"Talk to me, human."

"Whatever you say, wolf."

And I knew right then and there. Whatever he was going to say, I wasn't going to like it.

My wolf just might.

# CHAPTER 6

Jason

I HAD BEEN in a few precarious positions in my life as a geneticist who worked out in the field, but lying underneath a female wolf shifter while she pinned me to the ground and her claws wrapped around my throat was a new one.

I was friends with the Starlight Pack and worked with them on multiple projects. They trusted me with some of their most tangled secrets so that I could help them. I also knew Riaz decently well. We were drinking buddies. He liked me.

At least, that's what I assumed. I had never

met *this* particular wolf before, and the way that she growled at me, her eyes glowing gold while her claws pricked at my skin, I had a feeling that she probably never wanted to see me again.

This was going well.

The first time I saw a pretty woman in how long, and she wants to kill me.

And then I remembered the blood on my hands, on my chest, and froze. Because that wasn't my blood, and now I could remember *exactly* why I was here.

I cleared my throat. "I was on the trail of someone else." *Something* else. "I found this man here when I did. I thought I could save him, but somebody had already torn out his chest." I swallowed hard, and the woman above me, with dark hair and bright eyes, looked at me and tilted her head. It was such a wolf-like gesture it surprised me.

"Jason?" Rio asked from beside the woman above me, and I relaxed marginally, only marginally. After all, the woman above me still hadn't let go of my neck.

"You know him then?" she asked, her voice cold.

"I do. It took me a minute to scent him because of the blood." He let out a curse. "Jason, tell me you didn't fucking do this."

I stiffened, afraid even the idea of doing it would send this wolf on top of me over the edge. Guilt crept in at that since it wasn't only my life on the line. No, that man had died, and I hadn't been able to save him. "Of course I didn't. Do you see a weapon on me?"

"Then why the hell are you out here without a weapon? You say you're hunting rogues, and you don't bring anything? That doesn't sound like a brilliant thing to do." The woman shook her head, looked up at Rio, and then gave a tight nod. She stood up, letting go of my neck, and I barely resisted the urge to reach up and rub where she had touched, not because it had hurt, no, because I wanted to feel her warmth.

Well, that was a new weird quirk of mine. One I wasn't in the mood to deal with.

"What the fuck happened?" Rio asked as he held out his hand. I looked down at my bloody hands and winced.

"I don't know. I've been looking for evidence on the path of what we're trying to figure out, as part of what Riaz wanted me to look into, and I found him like this. I don't know who this is, though. I've never met him before. I don't think he was a rogue, was he? I don't know. I have too many questions. Not enough answers."

The woman looked at me then, her gaze penetrating.

"You work for the Alpha. Are you Pack?"

I shook my head as I met Rio's gaze, then Dane's. I

quickly lowered my eyes, as I didn't want to assert dominance. I was a human, and I honestly didn't know exactly how that worked. Would they try to push me down and prove that they were stronger than me? Because there was no need to do that. I knew where I would rank on the hierarchy, and it wasn't high. But I was smart, and I protected those that I loved. That had to count for something.

And now I was rambling. That's what happened when I was in situations that I didn't understand or quantify with math or science. I didn't know what had happened here, didn't know how I was supposed to fix things. And I didn't know what I was supposed to say around this woman. She made my brain short circuit, another thing that had never before happened in my life. I didn't think with my dick. I didn't even think with my heart. I thought with my mind. That was how I was supposed to be.

And yet, I couldn't focus.

It was all about her, those strong muscles, those curves that didn't quit.

Who the hell was this woman? And why couldn't I focus?

"This is Jason. He's a geneticist at the lab outside of the Pack. He's not part of our Pack, but he is a friend." Dane looked at me then, tilted his head in that wolf-like gesture again. "Though I don't know why he's out here alone without talking to us. You're on our territory, boy. There better be a damn good reason."

I swallowed hard. "I'm a geneticist. People are dying around here from a black blood cancer that we can't figure out. It's either forcing people to go rogue, or affecting their magic, or doing something. At least, that's what my colleagues think. What happens is it looks like a wolf bite, but with black marks. So I've been searching, trying to figure out exactly what's happening. I didn't think I'd find a rogue or this man." I swallowed hard. "I'm sorry. Was he your friend?"

The woman didn't say anything. She just stared at me. "I think I'm going to need to have a little more information." She turned to Dane, giving me her back. As if I wasn't a threat. And I wasn't, but it didn't make me feel any better about myself. "You're going to explain to me exactly what's going on down here."

"I don't answer to you, wolf."

"No. But our Alphas are trying to form an alliance. Do you think that keeping secrets is going to help that? I know the strength of your Pack, Dane. You don't want to make an enemy out of us."

The other wolf bristled. "Excuse me? You're all alone here, little girl. Watch it."

The woman moved so fast I could barely breathe.

Rio was in front of me, as if protecting me from what was going on, but then Dane was on his back, his hands up, and the woman hovered above him, her claws outstretched. This time she had pricked the other man's skin, a slight trickle of blood sliding down his neck. "You knew who was going to win that dominance challenge. And it wasn't you. We aren't Packmates. I understand that. I thought we were close to becoming allies. What the fuck is going on?"

"Let him up. Riaz told us we couldn't tell you unless something happened. And I guess this counts," Rio said, and I frowned, looking between them as if I was missing things.

"You don't get to tell me what to do, Rio, or you're going to be on your back too," the woman snapped.

"Kaylee, please," Rio whispered.

Kaylee. Her name is Kaylee.

I liked that.

And I wondered what the hell I cared about that for.

"Fine, for now, I'll let you up." She stood up, then held out her hand, and Dane let out a sharp laugh before taking it and letting her help him up.

"Well then, I guess you're not that much of an asshole if you're just going to help me up like that."

"I'm not an asshole at all. Nor am I a bitch. But you want to play dominance games? You deal with them. I might be small, but I can still kick your ass. All of your asses." She met my gaze, but this time I didn't pull away. Unlike with the guys, I didn't need to assert anything. There was nothing to pretend with her. I didn't know who she was or what was going on, but something was happening, something I needed to know more about.

Not that I had time for that.

"What about a blood cancer?" she asked as she nodded at me.

"I don't know what's going on with rogues. That's something that's another part of the problem. I'm searching for someone around here who is leaving black blood marks all over dead bodies. Something is killing witches and wolves, and I want to know what it is. I don't think it has to do with the rogue problem, other than someone's taking advantage of it. I think it's a two-pronged approach. I'm trying to find the root cause of it. Meaning, I aimed to come out here and try to see if I could find any answers. I didn't mean to find your man. I'm sorry. Was he yours?"

Kaylee raised her chin. "He was Pack. He was Spencer. And now he's dead. And you're covered in his blood."

"As I said, I was trying to save his life. I didn't realize I'd be too late."

"He's telling the truth. I don't smell a lie."

She tore her gaze from me and looked at Rio. "I can smell it just the same as you. But okay, I need to get Spencer home. I need to get him to his Pack."

"Wait," I cut in, and then cleared my throat as everybody stared at me. "I mean, I need to study him."

"Excuse me?" Kaylee asked, her eyes narrowing to slits. "He is not a lab specimen. You do not get to play with his body so that you can find out the secrets of our wolves. I don't know who you think you are or whatever pact you have with this Pack. You are not touching a hair on this man's head. He is Redwood. He is mine. You will walk away."

I swallowed hard and looked at the others.

"Let's talk to our Alphas," Rio whispered, and Kaylee cursed.

"You let him cut open your wolves? What secrets are you letting him know?"

"I'm not like that. I'm not a monster."

She met my gaze and growled. "I never said you were, but I've met the monsters. I know what they do. I've seen their depravities. You don't smell of darkness and sickness, but I don't know you. So why don't you take a fucking step back and let me think? Because you are not touching this man. You're not touching my Pack."

"I need to see what killed him. I want answers. For

all of us. I promise I will treat him with the respect and kindness that is owed to him. I promise you I'm not going to hurt him any more than he already was. Whoever's doing this is hurting my friends as well. I promise you I don't want to do anything that would jeopardize the treaties with your Pack or harm him at all."

"He's helping us figure out who is bringing on the black death."

"You already have a name for it?" she asked, her voice ice.

"No, that's the problem. We don't know what's going on. I'm not going to disgrace your wolf. I'm not going to learn your secrets. I promise you. I want to protect this Pack, and I want to make sure no one else gets hurt."

"I need to talk to my Alpha," she growled as she stared at me.

"We all will talk to our Alphas," Dane put in. "Jason is a friend of a Pack. He's a good man."

"And I don't know who he is," she whispered.

"You will," I promised, wondering why the hell I said that.

Both Rio and Dane gave me odd looks, but Kaylee just tilted her head, and a small smile played on her lips, but it didn't meet her eyes.

"Perhaps."

"But first, you're going to tell me exactly what the fuck is going on before I rip your throat out."

And even though I knew the warning was all truth, and the other wolves might try to stop her but wouldn't be able to, I couldn't help but wonder who the hell this woman was and why her strength turned me on.

And when I had turned into the lunatic I was becoming.

# CHAPTER 7

Jason

I COULDN'T STOP LOOKING at Kaylee Jamenson. There was no one like her. The fact that we were about to look at a dead body told me I shouldn't keep staring at her, but I wasn't able to stop. She'd glare at me, Rio and Dane would give me an odd look, but then I'd ignore them all and keep my gaze on her.

There was something genuinely wrong with me, and I wasn't sure what I was supposed to do about it.

"You're not Pack, but you work for them?" Kaylee asked, pulling me out of my thoughts.

I shook my head, doing my best not to stare. There's something wrong with me. We'd moved to my lab after we'd been introduced, and I still felt off. "I work with them sometimes, but my company doesn't work for the Pack. If that makes sense."

She studied me in that wolf way of hers, her gaze piercing, the gold showing slightly around her irises, as if her wolf was watching me too. Her head was tilted, her long hair falling over her shoulder. I wanted to reach out and touch that hair, to wrap it around my fist, to discover what it felt like.

Maybe I needed more sleep, or a fucking shower, since I was still covered in the other man's blood.

I swallowed hard, bile rising.

She looked at me then, reached forward, and grabbed my arm. "What's wrong?"

I froze, staring at her. "Why would you think something's wrong?" I asked, doing my best to keep my voice steady.

"You just looked pained. Is there something I need to know?"

"I'm fine. I was thinking about that man back there. My company may work with Riaz—so any rogues that they find that need someone beyond a healer to look at, we do, even though it's not a morgue—but you guys aren't humans, therefore, you don't have the exact laws and rules that we do."

"Meaning you're not used to dealing with dead bodies on a daily basis," she said softly, giving me a sad look. "Are you going to be okay?"

"He was your friend, or at least your Packmate. I should be the one asking you."

She met my gaze again, and unlike most wolves, I didn't feel the need to lower my eyes. I didn't think that was because she wasn't as dominant, though. There was a presence to her, a force. But I didn't need to lower my gaze at all, to bow to her dominance or feel afraid, as if I needed to show that I wasn't trying to threaten her or intimidate her.

"Spencer was a Packmate, and I didn't know him well, but I have lost friends. I've had to help pick their bodies up from the battlefield and help them be laid to rest with dignity."

"I'm sorry. Were you at the wars with the Centrals?" I asked, thinking of the battles that had happened between two warring Packs over thirty years ago. Now, not all of those wars and battles between Packs were common knowledge. I was close enough to the Starlight Pack that I knew more than others.

Kaylee snorted. "I was an infant during most of that, but thank you for not asking my age."

I winced. "A lot of the Starlight Pack wolves that I work with are either your age or nearly five hundred. It's hard to tell when you're a human. You know?"

"I can't usually tell the exact age of a wolf either, sometimes there's an age and a presence to them, but other times they surprise you by being a humorous dorky person who is nearly four hundred."

"So you must be referring to the time when we humans found out wolves existed."

She nodded. "That, and the other skirmish with the Aspens."

"I'm sorry you lost people."

"Thank you. It's never easy, and we still shouldn't be losing people after all this time. But my job is to make sure that we can find the people who are lost before it's too late." She swallowed hard, and I wanted to reach out, to tell her that I was sorry, but I had already done that, and that would make it more awkward.

"Anyway, while Spencer's family is here, his Pack is with the Redwoods, up north with me. So, I will talk to my Alpha and his family to see what I'll do next."

"I'll help you with whatever you need," I said.

"You found him, and I should probably apologize for tossing you to the ground."

My cheeks heated and I shrugged, rubbing the back

of my neck with my hand. "No, it's fine. It did look a little odd me standing over him like that." I swallowed hard again, my stomach rolling.

"So, you're working with the rogues? I mean to find them."

I nodded, grateful to go back to what I was good at. Science. Talking about science—not so much because that would require talking to other people and especially a beautiful woman, and I wasn't that great at that, but I was learning.

"Come on, Rio said that they would be moving Spencer in here, and then we can take some blood samples and see what I can do. I'll treat him with the utmost respect."

She let out a small growl, then I froze.

"I know you will because I'll be standing beside you the whole time. The others may trust you, but I don't know you. You seem nice, and while I do apologize for throwing you on the ground, I would do it again and again at that moment. My Packmate is dead. I don't know you. I don't know this Pack. And while I am grateful for how kind you are being, I want to know what happened."

I nodded, swallowing hard. "I want to know what happened too. The problem is two-fold. There are rogues that are increasing, at least from what Riaz said. I don't have the data on that, to tell you the truth."

"Okay."

She wasn't going to give an inch, and for that, I respected her. I wasn't Pack, I didn't need to know the ins and outs, but I needed to know enough.

"The other problem is these bite marks. There is something being injected into them or attacking them that isn't like anything I've seen. Maybe you have, as there isn't just a nice Pack archive I could look up research and problems that have arisen in the past."

"Yes, because putting up all of our illnesses and weaknesses for the government to see seems like a great idea," she said dryly.

"First, I'm not the government. Second, I would never share that information outside of this group."

"There are ways to get information out of people, Jason."

Why did this woman saying my name like that do things to me? There was something seriously fucking wrong with me.

"I'm not going to say anything. I promise you."

"I don't know you well enough to see if that promise makes any sense." I met her gaze and gave her a tight nod. She didn't trust me, but I wanted her to. I wanted to know more about her.

She took a step forward, as if against her own voli-tion, and she frowned, shaking her head. "What the hell is wrong with me?" she muttered, and I had to wonder the same thing about myself.

This wasn't a usual thing for me. I wasn't great around women, it took me a while to get through my awkwardness, but I wasn't usually this drawn to another, especially under these circumstances.

"How many bodies have you found like this?" she asked as we got to my desk, and I pointed at a few files at her.

"Around here? Eleven."

The tablet dropped from her hand and she reached out quickly to catch it before it fell, and she blinked. "Eleven?"

"In the state. There could be more around the US, but I don't know. We're searching."

"Eleven. Eleven people with these black bite marks?"

"Yes. Over the past two years."

"And why haven't I heard about this? Why hasn't anyone heard about this?"

"Because Riaz said to keep it private."

She narrowed her eyes. "And you just listened to the Alpha?"

"He's a very large wolf with very sharp teeth. Of

course I fucking listened to the Alpha."

Her gaze widened at my profanity, but I shrugged. "He's helping. The whole Pack is. And it's not just wolves this is happening to. There are humans too, and a witch."

"Why hasn't this hit the news? Why does no one know what's going on?"

"Because nobody put it together until recently."

She blinked. "You. You put it together recently."

"As of two weeks ago, I put it together. Nobody was talking to one another, and Texas is a fucking big state. They didn't put two and two together until I started looking into the death of a local wolf."

"So it's going to break soon."

"It might. But people still don't know what's going on; my goal is to figure out what the hell is going on so I can help the Pack find this person or wolf or whatever."

"Damn it. I need to call my Pack. They need to know."

"You should talk to Riaz first."

A low growl rumbled in her throat. "Riaz is not my Alpha. Spencer was a Redwood. I'm telling my Alpha and my Pack what the fuck is going on down here. They can help. I can help. Because I'm going to find out what happened to him."

"Okay then. I'm not Pack, I'm not going to get in the middle of that."

"Good."

She let out a breath, her shoulders shaking. I frowned and then moved forward without even thinking. I put my hand on her shoulder, and she froze.

"What's wrong?"

"I'm fine."

But she wasn't fine. I could hear it in her voice.

I looked at Spencer's photo. One of him looking happy and smiling.

Riaz had given me Spencer's file that morning, and now here Kaylee was, looking down at the Packmate that was no longer here with us, the Packmate that's body was in the next room, the Packmate that I had been leaning over covered in blood.

And without thinking, I pulled Kaylee close and held her.

"I'm sorry." She stiffened for a moment before she wrapped her arms around my waist and let out a shuddering breath. We stood there, for how long I didn't know, but she breathed into me, and I had to wonder why this felt right, why this felt like we had done this a thousand times.

She pulled away after a few minutes and let out a

shaky breath. "Thank you. I think my wolf is missing my Pack. I appreciate it."

Her words sounded true, yet there was something else there, something I didn't know.

But this wasn't the time to ask.

With the way things were going, I didn't think it ever would be.

# CHAPTER 8

Kaylee

WHO THE HELL was this man, and why couldn't I focus?

I let out a breath and told myself that this wasn't the time. I was here to find Spencer. And now I needed to find out what had happened to him and who had done this to him.

I didn't have another choice, nor did I want one.

I needed answers, and so did Spencer's family.

So did my Pack.

Jason looked at me before he pushed his hair back from his face and frowned.

"I'm sorry."

I tilted my head, staring at him, my wolf prowling, wanting more. Wanting anything.

Who was this man, and why was he doing this to me?

"Sorry for what?"

"For holding you like that. You don't even know me."

I shook my head. "No, we don't know each other, but my wolf needed it. We're tactile. Thank you. I just can't believe this is how I found him."

He looked at me then, swallowed hard once more. "I'm sorry. About your friend. About everything. It shouldn't have happened this way. I need to know everything I can of how you think he got down here and what you think he was doing down here."

"I don't know, he was supposed to be in Philly, and then he wasn't. So I want to know what happened. And why he came down here in the first place."

"Maybe the family? Do you think he turned rogue?"

I sighed. "That's my problem. We're not going to be able to tell unless you do the autopsy."

"We'll get that done."

"A genetics lab will get that done?" I asked.

"It's part of the same company that works with the

Packs. We have our own rules. And we'll treat him with respect."

"We'll see about that." I narrowed my eyes. "I won't have him be disrespected."

"Understandable. I wouldn't want you to. But if he didn't turn rogue, then he came here for help."

"Or someone chased him down here."

"Maybe. Are you going to stay and find out?" he asked, an odd catch in his tone.

I nodded. "Yes. I need to find out what happened to my Packmate and why someone would hurt him. Along the way, I want to find out what this black mark is. And who attacked my Packmate. Because even if he had gone rogue, someone hurt him. Someone attacked him. And I want to know who it was."

"Then I'll help. Whatever I do, I'll help."

"Good," I said, then I shook myself. "I need to call my Alpha. Tell him what happened."

"Do you want me in the room?"

I studied him then, and my wolf didn't want him to go. If I was honest with myself, the human half didn't want him to leave either.

Something was here, something between us, and that could be a problem. Because I didn't know him, but my wolf wanted to know more about him. That worried me. It worried me way more than I thought possible. Who was this man, and why did I want to throw myself at him and rub against him until everyone smelled me on him and knew he was mine? I didn't want anyone to get the idea that they could come near him. I wanted to claim him as my own so that way no one would dare go near my territory. I blinked and held back a curse. No, that couldn't be it. I was just attracted to him, and it was in an odd time and place. There was no way that this could be what I thought it was. I pushed the thoughts from my mind because I didn't have time for them, and Spencer needed me to focus on him and not focus on my needs, whatever they may be.

"I'm going to call now. See what they want me to do. I want to stay, and I know that they will want me to, but I want to confirm."

"Okay. I'll tell them whatever they need to know. Riaz already said that I could."

I raised a brow. "And the Alpha of the Starlight Pack would, what, hold me back from telling my own Alpha?"

"Stop. That's not what I said. I just don't know the mechanics and everything. I'm not a Packmate."

"No, but you seem to know a lot about wolves."

"I happen to know as much as I do because I work with Riaz and Rio and the others. But I only know as much as they tell me what I can glean from the news."

My hackles rose. "You mean what the human media dares to tell you about those savage wolves?" I asked, my voice a growl.

He shook his head. "No. What wolves tell us on the news. I was always on your side when it came to what the government did to you. When they tried to put collars on you and claim that you weren't human enough in order to deny you any rights. If I was a fighter at all, I would have fought alongside the Pack. As it was, I hid two young adult wolves who were at school with me during that war. I was teaching a biology course on campus, and they were my students. I hid them in my office when those military types were out to hunt them."

He had such a growl in his voice, his eyes narrow and bright as he said it, that my wolf pushed at me, wanting close. I hadn't even realized I had taken a step closer to him until it was too late.

"They tried to take the wolves?" I asked, my voice low, dangerous.

Jason swallowed hard, his jaw tense. "Yes. I hid them and led them away and made sure Riaz knew his wolves were here. They protected them. Just like I tried to. These were kids. Twenty years old and getting their damn degrees so they could help their Pack and the others. They wanted to be doctors, for humans and wolves, and look what happened, some fucking commandos show up with guns threatening to take these kids. No, I wasn't going to have any of that."

"What happened to these commandos?" I asked, my voice even lower.

"I'm not sure, they went away to search for others, and I tried to warn people, but it wasn't like you guys told us who you were. And I didn't want you guys to have markers to point yourselves out. But I did my best to let those I knew who would be of my like mind to protect others. And then that whole serum thing came out, and things got complicated."

I froze. "You know of the serum thing?"

"I only know because I was part of the team to help destroy what we found," he said softly.

"What serum are you talking of." I knew what serum he might be talking about, but in case he thought it was something else, I wasn't going to enlighten him.

"The one that a certain former general was trying to create in order to make his own wolves."

"I see."

"You don't need to elaborate," he said, letting out a breath. "I know you have your secrets to protect your people, and I understand it. But I was on the team to help destroy it so that way nobody else could use it as a weapon. I heard that somebody was able to survive through it, but only by special means. I don't even know what those means are. My job was to destroy it, not study it and break it open and try to recreate it. Riaz wouldn't let me survive if that was the case."

He spoke of his execution as if it was natural, and honestly, in our world, it was.

"Why aren't you Pack?"

"I've not mated into the Pack. I have no family members that are part of it. It always just made sense for me to be close to it, but never part of it. Riaz said that he could blood me into the Pack if I wanted to, to create a bond, but you know the rules, you're not allowed to make wolves."

I let out a growl. "It was our own moral compass, but now it's become law thanks to our treaties with the humans."

"So even if I wanted to, they can't change me into a wolf unless I'm near death. And as I have no plans to be near death, here we are. However, that was a long-winded explanation of my saying you're safe here. Now, call your Alpha if you'd like."

"Fine."

I pulled out my phone and called quickly. Kade answered on the first ring. "Kaylee? Are you okay?"

"I'm fine. But there are a few things you need to know."

I outlined finding Spencer's body, the possible rogue situation, and the black marks. Jason added a few things as I spoke, and Kade paused. "Is this human with you then?"

"His name is Jason," I corrected, a slight growl in my voice. I held it back as much as I could though, because this was my Alpha, my uncle, and my superior.

It was hard not to be the asshole in this situation.

"He's safe."

And though I had been the one to drill and question Jason, I didn't want anybody else to do the same.

I didn't know what this meant, and I didn't want to. But there was something here, and I needed to focus.

Even if it meant ignoring things that were important.

"Okay. I have plans on speaking with Riaz right after this. Do you want to stay there, Kaylee? To get justice for Spencer?"

"Yes. I want to find out who did this. And I want to find out more of why Spencer was here."

"From what Nick has been able to tell, Spencer got a phone call from his old home and came back to Texas rather than go to the conference. But that's all he could find out."

"When did he find this out, and why didn't I know it?" I asked, feeling hurt at the slight.

"About three minutes before you called. If you hadn't called me, I was going to call you. You're doing a great job, Kaylee. I hate the fact that our Packmate is dead. That I didn't feel the severing of our bond until recently."

I cursed. "You already knew he was dead when I called."

"Of course I did. The hierarchy is all connected to you, and so we did. But I wanted to confirm because, for all I knew, he was just severed from the Pack and not life itself. He will be mourned here, his life celebrated. But his family is down there as well, and hopefully the answers are too. So stay as long as you need." He paused. "I can't send Connor, he has things to do up here, but do you want me to send your dad? Nico?"

I shook my head and then remembered he couldn't see me. "No, I can do this. I'm working with a few of the Starlight Pack. And Jason."

"Jason then?" he growled, his voice low. Even though Jason wasn't wolf and wouldn't be able to hear, with the way that my cheeks flushed he did raise a brow.

"Thank you for trusting me to do this. I'll give you an answer soon, Uncle Kade."

"I like that I'm Uncle Kade and not Alpha when I'm

teasing you about a certain man who seems to put a nice growl into your voice."

"I'm hanging up now."

"If that's what you say."

"Tell Mom I said hi."

"Oh, I'm going to be telling her a few other things."

I held back a snort, amazed I could even laugh at the situation.

Spencer was dead. We needed to find out who had called him here and why someone wanted him dead. We needed answers, and yet all I could do was wonder about the man beside me and why my Alpha and uncle had picked up on something in my voice I hadn't even realized was there.

"I'm staying," I said as I slid my phone into my pocket.

Jason looked at me then, his broad shoulders hovering over me, and he swallowed hard. I watched the long lines of his neck and told myself I wasn't going to give in. I wasn't going to listen to my wolf.

Because I had never felt this pull before, never felt this need.

And I was truly afraid that I had done the one thing I hadn't been prepared for.

But Jason just stared, "Good. I'm glad you're going to be here."

His voice soothed my wolf, and I held back a curse.

This couldn't be it. This couldn't be him.

I couldn't have just found my mate. A human. Long from home.

And in the one situation that could mean both of our deaths.

# CHAPTER 9

Jason

I HAD NEVER BEEN INVITED to a Pack funeral before, and I wasn't sure what I was supposed to think about it. I stood by Kaylee's side, on the other side of Rio, glancing at Spencer's parents as they held each other close, both so stoic I was afraid if they dropped a single tear, they'd never be whole again.

I could practically taste the anger and sorrow in the air. The fact that nobody knew exactly why we had lost Spencer or who had attacked him angered so many people. I could sense it. You could hear it in the rumblings between all of them as they spoke to one another.

I was terrified that whoever had killed Jason would do it again.

They would find Kaylee or someone else tracking the killer, and it would be the end for them.

I needed to find the monster, whatever form they may be, and try to find a way to stop them. This monster was leaving behind black bite marks, bite marks that could end a person's life.

I had never seen it before, and while I was still new to the paranormal world, the fact that Riaz wanted me to work so closely with them told me that they were worried as well.

I was still looking for clues as to what could be doing this, what could be causing this, but I was focusing on the sorrow in front of me for now. Kaylee hadn't moved, hadn't said a word. She stood there, stoic, as if she blamed herself for what had happened. I didn't know her well, but without thinking, I reached out and gripped her hand. She froze, looked down to where I touched her, and I wanted to pull back, only I didn't. Instead, she threaded her fingers with mine, squeezed, and didn't let go. I didn't know what it meant, I didn't know what it should mean, but it didn't matter. In that moment, as Spencer's parents did their best not to break down in front of the rest of us, I held Kaylee's hand and wondered why I felt so connected to her when I didn't even know her.

"We lost Spencer in an act of brutality and uncertainty. He came here for a reason, and we will find out who it was that killed him and why he'd come in the first place. What happened. All of us will. The Redwood Pack Alpha will also hold a moment of time for Spencer. For a Pack member who has been with them for nearly forty years, for a Pack member that they lost, whose bond is severed in a way that cannot be taken back. Spencer was ours for the first twenty years of his life. He was ours."

Riaz raised his chin. "And now he is gone. He will be buried amongst the mountains and trees in his beloved Redwood Forest. And his parents will go with him to that place with the Redwoods, and we will be sending an envoy as well. We might not be true allies in the sense of the word, but the Redwoods are our brothers and sisters. They have lost theirs as much as we have lost ours."

I squeezed Kaylee's hand but she didn't look at me. Instead, she leaned slightly into me, and I wondered again why I was there. Why I had the honor of being invited, even as it felt like sorrow crashed around me.

"We will go to the Redwoods, and we will have

answers." Riaz looked at me then, and I raised my chin. He was the Alpha, and I couldn't meet his gaze, but I could look right at his eyebrow, so he knew I wasn't going to back down. I wasn't a submissive, and I was human and could walk away, but I wasn't going to challenge him.

Riaz gave me a tight nod then looked at Kaylee. "Kaylee is here from the Redwoods, she will find who did this. We were too late. I refuse to be too late again. But, I will not let this day be drenched in sorrow. Now we will speak of Spencer, the boy we knew and the young man who moved on to another world. And then we will mourn. First, let us sing the song of those we have lost."

The wolves around me in human form threw their heads back and howled, an eerily beautiful howl that made the hair on the back of my neck and arms stand on end.

Kaylee looked at me as she finished, and I'd never seen anyone so beautiful. She was gorgeous and made my mouth water, even if I knew that this wasn't the time or the place.

Nor would it ever be, since she didn't live here, and I didn't have any plans on leaving my home.

Why had that thought entered my mind? It didn't make any sense.

I pushed those thoughts away as Riaz began to speak, and then the others did the same. They all moved around, speaking to one another when the large wolf I knew as Tristan came forward. He sidled up to Kaylee and looked her up and down.

"You're a Tracker then?" Tristan asked, and I bristled, the same as Kaylee.

"I am. I'm sorry for your loss." She let out a breath. "Our loss."

"While you're here, if you need to work off some of that aggression, I'm here for you." He winked, and I blinked at the gall of him. I hadn't even realized I had stepped forward, a human growl escaping out of my throat.

"You think this is the time or the place?" I asked, and Kaylee let out a huff of breath behind me.

"You're a human in a wolf's world. I think I'd learn my place."

And then Tristan walked off and Kaylee snorted behind me. "I can take care of myself. Especially against overbearing, arrogant men."

"I didn't realize he was such an asshole," I grumbled.

"I don't know if he really is. He might not like humans for some reason or another, but we're all hurting. That's what happens when you lose someone you care about."

"I'm sorry. That you lost someone."

"I'm sorry too. We will avenge him. We will find out the reason. But don't stand up for me like that. I may be a woman, but I am a dominant wolf. And you're lucky I wasn't growly just then. I've already thrown you on your back in the dirt once. I'll do it again."

And why did that turn me on? Maybe I'd hit my head when she'd done that.

I sighed. "So we're going to a search for this murderer then?"

"There's no we about it. You're going to find out what this monster is, and you're never going to go out hunting."

"Excuse me?" I asked, figurative hackles raised.

"You heard me. You're human. And I realize that my father is human as well, and he can fight better than some of the wolves I know, but I don't know anything about you. I don't know what you can do. However, everyone else says you're brilliant, so let's use that. Seriously. Use that. Find out what is causing these mutations or whatever the hell they are, and we'll find out who murdered him."

"Because Spencer wasn't rogue."

She shook her head. "He wasn't. Someone lured him out here and murdered him. I don't know why. But I'm going to find out. And then I'm going to end them."

I met her gaze, her eyes glowing gold.

"And what if it's connected to whatever is going on with the black bite marks?"

"Then we'll take care of that too. Protect the people here and anyone who's close to my Pack. We lost Spencer. I refuse to lose anyone else."

"Even if you get hurt in the process?"

"I'm a wolf, a Tracker. I'm going to get hurt. But I hurt them right back. And I'm not going to let anyone hurt you, Jason."

I blinked. "You're so sure of that?"

"I'm not sure of anything right now, but when I make a promise, I keep it."

And then she turned on her heel, and I couldn't help but watch her away.

Riaz came up to me, followed my gaze, and sighed.

"Be careful."

"You're warning me away from her?"

"No, but everyone's going to be high on adrenaline for a while, and she's a dominant wolf."

"And what, I'm just a weak little human?" I asked with a growl.

"I'm not saying that. But if you're going to play, make sure you hold on for one hell of a ride."

Riaz shook his head, then moved over to talk with another set of wolves, and I just stared at the others, wondering once again why I had been invited and why the Pack seemed to surround me.

I didn't know them. They didn't know me.

I didn't have a family anymore. I had lost them right when I turned eighteen. It was just me, my colleagues, and whatever I could come up with to try to help the people around me.

The Pack was all I had, and I didn't really have them.

And yet, something pushed me towards Kaylee. And I wanted to find out what it was.

Even if I knew that taking that step, listening to the voice inside my head say it was okay to take a chance, would be a mistake.

After all, she didn't live here. And I wasn't a man for just one night.

And Kaylee wasn't a woman that I was ever going to be able to forget.

Even if perhaps I should.

# CHAPTER 10

Kaylee

I DIDN'T HAVE time for this. Nobody did. I needed to find out who killed Spencer. Who had lured him down here and taken his life.

I rubbed my chest before I began to pace my small hotel room.

I had been so close to finding Spencer. Just a few moments earlier and perhaps I would have been able to save him. My wolf tugged at me, pain radiating through her. The same pain that arched through me. I was a Tracker. It was my job to find those who were lost, taken, or who threatened our Pack. The fact that I hadn't been able to find him until it was too late would forever haunt me. How was I supposed to face my Alpha, my family, while knowing I hadn't been enough to protect him? I had lost him.

I wasn't sure what I was supposed to do now.

And I surely should not be thinking about Jason every time I took a breath. I knew who he could be. What he was to me.

My mate. The one person for me, the one person I could be with until the end of my days.

And yet, I couldn't let this happen. I didn't even know him, yet my wolf kept prowling at me. In fact, she paced within me, crawling, wanting to know more about this human who seemed to be a friend of the Pack, who seemed to know so much about our people. The Starlight Pack trusted him; I could tell that much. They trusted him with their secrets, even more than they trusted me, being an outsider wolf who was there to find a dead former Packmate of theirs.

Who was this Jason? Was mating supposed to be like this? I didn't like the fact that I seemed to be so out of control with my own feelings and wants. I should be able to think logically through any feelings I had for this stranger, and yet I couldn't.

He stood up for me against Tristan, against anyone

who thought that they could have me because I was a lone female among them. It didn't matter that I could handle myself and I didn't need Jason to protect me. My wolf had liked it, and I didn't even understand that. My wolf hated when men thought that they needed to take care of the little woman and stepped up for me to the point that I didn't have a choice. My wolf was not that kind to men who thought they knew better than me. And yet, it wasn't like that with Jason. My wolf had chosen, had decided that, yes, that was the man for me, and yet when did I get the choice? When did I get the ability to make my own decisions? It didn't make any sense.

My family had always discussed mating and what it could mean for people in our family. No one in my immediate family had found their mates, though many of my cousins had. However, we all knew the story of the triad and how they had come to be.

They had nearly died protecting each other, and had saved the Pack along the way.

I wasn't sure how I was supposed to live up to that, or even if I wanted to.

I wasn't sure how I found my own place within that. I wanted to have my own strength, my own choice, and yet my wolf wanted him—that man.

There was a knock at the door that shook me out of

my thoughts and I froze, scenting the wolf on the other side.

Riaz. The Alpha.

I let out a growl and stalked to the door, opening it, wondering why he was in my space. Yes, I was on his territory, but this was my space. I didn't like dominant Alphas in my way.

And yet, why did I like Jason? He wasn't submissive, and he was human, and yet my body apparently wanted more.

What was wrong with me?

"I wanted to see if you had everything you need," Riaz said, in lieu of greeting.

I raised my chin, though I didn't meet his gaze. I wasn't in the mood for a dominance battle, and obviously I knew I wouldn't win. I was strong, but not Alpha strong.

"I do. Thank you. I need to meet with Jason soon to discuss a few things, and then I'll be on the hunt."

"Yeah, whatever you need from us. We need to find out who did this to Spencer, and more about these black bite marks."

I nodded. "Okay. I'm going to do whatever I can. I refuse to even allow the idea that I won't find this traitor. This attacker."

"What makes you think it's a traitor?"

He tilted his head as he said it, curious, and I relaxed. He wasn't trying to prove his dominance, wasn't trying to take over. He was genuinely curious. I didn't know much about this Alpha, but I liked him, which surprised me.

"I meant more so traitor to our way, not where he came from. Or they. I'm not even sure what's exactly is going on, but I will figure it out. My Alpha has given me leave to stay here until I do."

"And we welcome you as a guest to the Pack, Kaylee Jamenson. Is it okay if I send Dane and Rio with you for most of this?"

"I don't mind."

Honestly, I didn't. Of many of the wolves that I had met, they were the least annoying, even though I had growled a bit with Dane. Rio was nice, a little sweeter, but he probably held that edge hidden, where he would just come out and slash at whoever came at him.

"Good then. Do you know where Jason lives?"

"He gave me his address."

"Well then. I need to go meet with the elders, but I'm here if you need me." He tilted his head again. "I would have said if you need help with anything, but I do believe I know exactly where you'll go to ask for help."

He winked as he said it, then left, and I held back a growl.

I was pretty sure I'd just been propositioned by an Alpha, by not being propositioned by him.

He knew I had found my mate.

And damn it, what was I supposed to do about it?

My nipples hardened and I squeezed my thighs together, annoyed that just the thought of Jason brought me to that need. This damn mating urge. This is not what I needed right then.

You do not fall for your mate at first glance. You needed time. You needed to walk through your life together and see if they work.

This wasn't the time of my parents when mating just happened, and things worked out. It couldn't be.

And yet, it seems that's what my wolf wanted.

I wasn't my wolf, though. I picked up my bag and headed out of the hotel room, going to the rental car that I had gotten from the Pack. Dane and Rio were nowhere to be found, so I assumed they gave me the lead to head to Jason's on my own. Maybe they were already there. I didn't know. They would find me if they needed to. This was their territory, after all. It is what I would do in their place.

I made my way across Pack territory to a set of apart-ments along the edge. I could sense Jason around, and that worried me. There were other humans everywhere, even a few witches and a couple of wolves that seemed to live in this apartment building. And yet, I could pick Jason's scent out of all of them.

Damn it.

Growling, annoyed at my wolf's needs and the fact that the human part of me seemed to want to follow far too earnestly, I slammed the door behind me and snarled my way through the apartment building. One submissive wolf gave me a look and then lowered their head quickly, fear wafting off them. I cursed under my breath, hating myself.

"I'm sorry. I'm in a bad mood. It has nothing to do with you. I'm truly sorry. I'm Kaylee. From the Redwoods."

The wolf looked up at me then, not meeting my gaze, but the fear dissipated quickly.

"Oh, I'm Heath. I'm mated to Alice, one of Riaz's lieutenants."

I nodded, my wolf coming forward, interested in this dynamic.

"And you live here then? You don't have to answer that," I said quickly, holding up my hands. "I was just interested."

"Oh, no worries. I'm tutoring somebody that lives in the apartment building. We live in the den, since Alice is lieutenant and we need to be near. I guess you're here visiting Jason?" Heath asked, the teasing lilt to his tone telling me that he was a submissive and fearful of the dominant wolf scowling through the hallways, but he also had a backbone of steel.

I liked him already.

And I would do anything to protect him. Not just because he was a submissive, but because the way he said Jason's name told me that they knew each other and that they were friends.

I have no idea why my wolf told me these things, but I trusted her.

And God forbid any rogue or transformed wolf or whatever was causing these black marks came at Heath.

That was what made me a dominant, the need to protect those in my purview—those weaker than me.

"I am," I said slowly, trying to pull myself out of my own rage.

"Well, he is there. He came home from whatever he was doing when I was finishing up my tutoring."

"Do you have somebody to take you back to the den? It's not safe right now."

"My mate's on her way," he said with a smile. "I swear all you dominant wolves are the same. All about protection and growling."

"Perhaps, but maybe I'll wait here until your mate gets here."

I didn't have to wait long, the scent of dominant

female wolf wafting through the air as Alice came towards me.

I hadn't seen her at the funeral, but I recognized her scent. She had been on patrol, and that's where I had remembered sensing her before.

"Kaylee. I'm Alice."

She raised her chin but didn't meet my gaze. I didn't think it was a sign of submission, only that we didn't have time for dominance games. Me being an unknown wolf in their territory meant that things got complicated when trying to figure out who fit where in the hierarchy.

"Kaylee was just here protecting me since I was standing all alone in this hallway."

"You were supposed to be in the apartment until I got here," Alice teased, before she leaned down and kissed her mate hard on the mouth. It was a sensual kiss, one meant for the bedroom and not public spaces, but I didn't mind. They looked happy.

I could be that happy. If I just gave in.

And no, I wasn't going to think about that.

"Thanks for watching out for him. Between traffic and the shit week that we've had, I was late."

"No, you weren't. I was early." He sighed. "And I know everyone's on edge. That's why I'm not allowed to be left alone, like a little toddler, but I can protect myself." He held up his clawed fingertips. "See? I'm a big boy wolf and everything." He rolled his eyes, kissed his mate on the mouth, and then tugged her towards the door. "Jason's waiting for you. Go meet with him."

"Jason, is it?" Alice teased, before she gave me a finger wave and headed out with her mate.

I shook my head, feeling oddly jealous over the easiness the two had with one another.

I could have that. Couldn't I? No. Not here. Not now. I needed to find who killed Spencer. And then I needed to go home.

Jason was here, not where I came from.

I didn't have time for a mate. I didn't have time to lose control.

Yet why did I feel like I wasn't doing anything right?

I made my way upstairs, and before I could knock on the door, Jason opened it, a smile on his face. "I heard you guys downstairs. Thin walls."

I shook my head at the flimsy door lock and scowled. "This isn't a great place for you to be living for security."

"There's always a wolf on duty, and since I'm saving up for a house, that means I get this rat hole. Sorry." He stepped back, letting me duck my head, blushing.

"I'm sorry. I wasn't the one that called it a rat hole, though."

"It's not the best of apartments, it's nice, but it's not

the greatest. And yes, I do rely on the Pack security, sue me."

"I'm glad that they take care of you. And all of their people." The Starlight Pack seemed healthy from the outside and, so far, everything I was learning spoke to that nature. I just hoped that was the truth, since they wanted an allyship with my Pack.

Jason closed the door behind me, locking it, and my wolf growled, a need hitting me like a freight train.

He studied me, his eyes going dark, his mouth part-ing, and I lost all sense.

Clearly I had, because that was the only reason that I moved forward.

The only reason.

I pressed my hands into his shoulders and growled low.

"Tell me no."

"Never," Jason said, surprising us both. And then I lowered my lips to his, and I kissed him.

# CHAPTER 11

Jason

I GROANED, her taste nearly sending me over the edge. I couldn't breathe, couldn't think. All I wanted was her.

My hand slid into her hair, tugging slightly as her hands scraped down my back. I knew she was using her fingernails, not claws, but even the thought of that happening made me groan. I turned us so her back was to the door, and I shoved her hard, kissing her, needing her. She nipped at my lip and I groaned again, kissing along the edge of her jaw, then down her neck.

Kissing her like this, without regard for what could

happen next, was crazy. This couldn't be happening. We both needed to stop, and yet neither one of us was going to.

She shoved her hand up my shirt, her palms over my skin, and I groaned, needing more.

I slid one hand over the back of her neck, tilting her head so I could kiss her deeper, the other going up her shirt to cup her breast. She had her hand down my pants, gripping my ass as we both ground into one another, kissing each other harder and harder.

Her lace-covered breast filled my palm and I slid my thumb over her nipple, the pebbled nub pressing into my thumb.

I pinched, just a little bit, and she gasped, wrapping one leg around my hip as her heat pressed against my jean-clad cock.

I was already too hard, ready to break, and yet all I wanted to do was go deeper and keep kissing her.

Her hand slid to the front of my jeans, cupping me, and I grumbled, squeezing my eyes together as she slid her hand over my length. I moved, jostling us both as I slid my hand away from her breast and down her pants. She was hot, wet, and sweet. I spread her folds, playing with her clit as both of us kissed harder, panting, needing.

And then I realized what the fuck I was doing.

I was nearly ready to come in my jeans with Kaylee's hand around my dick, my hand down her pants, and almost ready to plunge into her and make her come, her cunt pulsating around my fingers.

I cursed, ripped my hand from her pants, and took a stifling step back, trying to calm myself, trying to collect my thoughts.

"What the fuck was that?" I asked, my voice a snarl.

All I wanted to do was put my fingers to my lips and suck her wetness off them, but I didn't. I couldn't.

Her gaze went to my hand, and fuck it. I looked at her then, stuck my fingers in my mouth, and sucked her sweet tartness off my fingers.

Her eyes glowed gold, her wolf at the forefront, and I nearly came at the taste of her.

I had never been this person. Never this brazen or whatever the fuck I was just then, and I didn't care.

This was Kaylee, a woman I didn't even know, and now I had her on my lips.

"What the fuck was that?" I asked again, my hand down at my side, my chest heaving. My dick was so hard I was afraid I would burst in my jeans, but I told myself that I was fine. That I could handle myself. That I had control.

And I wasn't sure that was actually the case.

"I'm sorry."

I looked at Kaylee and blinked. "You're sorry? I'm the one that attacked you." Guilt and shame spread over me, and I cursed under my breath. "I pawed at you."

"Is that some kind of shifter joke?" she asked, a brow raised.

I rolled my eyes. "No. It's me saying I literally attacked you against the door."

"I'm the one that kissed you first, if you don't remember. I'm not saying I didn't like it," she growled out.

"Oh?" I asked, confused as ever. "I've never...not with anyone."

"Are you telling me you're a virgin?" she asked, her eyes wide.

I ran my hand through my hair, cursing once more. "I'm not saying that. *Seriously* not saying that. All I'm saying is I've never kissed another person quite like that, ever. With so much need, and the fact that I don't even know who you are. I know your name. I know your position in the Pack. I know where you're from, but that's it. So why do I feel that I've known you my entire life, or that I've been waiting to know you?" I rubbed at my chest, annoyed at myself. "Why do I feel like I should know more?"

"Jason," she whispered, and her voice went straight

through me, the need surprising me, the ache making me want.

My hands shook, and I took a deep breath. "I feel like I took advantage of you, that I forced you into that."

Kaylee's eyes filled with gold again, and she shook her head. "You didn't do anything I didn't ask for. I'm the one who started it. I clawed at you, remember?"

"And yet, I shoved you against the door."

She looked at me then, her head tilted in her wolf way. "I liked it. I'm a wolf. So it looks like neither one of us took advantage of each other." She let out a deep breath and shook her head.

"What's that look for?" I asked. "If neither one of us took advantage of each other, what is that look for?"

"We should get back to the data. So you can show me exactly what you mean by these bite marks and what you've been looking for all this time."

"You're not going to get out of it that easily."

"Excuse me?" she asked, that wolfish tone of hers making me grin. I liked the way she sounded. The way that she made me grin just by that growl in her voice.

"I don't want to go over bite marks and rogue wolves or whoever is causing this. I want to know why we just attacked each other like that, and why I feel like I could do it for hours, and that was just the beginning. Just a single taste."

"We don't have time for this, Jason. I don't have time for this. I need to find out what happened to my Pack-mate and who killed him. Don't you understand that? You might have been too late to save him, but what about me? My job was to find him, to track him down, and yet I couldn't. I wasn't strong enough. I wasn't good enough. He's dead, and we were so close to finding him, and yet not close enough. He is gone, and now I'm sitting here kissing you and wanting more? No, I'm not that wolf. I will never be that wolf."

I lifted my chin, understanding and hating myself for forgetting for just an instant why she was here. Not that I could actually forget. Not that the nightmares of finding Spencer as I had would ever fully leave my brain, but at that moment, I had let myself be.

And she had so much guilt over that, and I didn't blame her. Because I was feeling the same. And I hadn't even known the other man.

"I'm sorry. You're right. I should be focusing on that. On Spencer. On the eleven souls that we lost. I'm sorry."

She gave me a look, one that I couldn't read, before she cursed under her breath and ran her hands through that gorgeous mane of hers. "It's not your fault. Not really."

"I am sorry."

"Please don't say that. We can't be sorry for what happened, but we can't let it happen again."

"Will you at least tell me why?"

I had a feeling I knew, even though I shouldn't, even though it didn't make any sense.

"Don't ask me that, Jason."

"I think I need to. I think you need to say it out loud."

"Fine. You want to know? The Moon Goddess has declared that you could be my mate. That we could be mates. That we could be the perfect people for one another and create a bond. That's the mating urge between us that you feel. The need? It doesn't go away. It gets stronger and stronger until one of us finally breaks and walks away forever, or we lean into one another. All I want to do is strip you down and take you and mark you as mine. All I want is to lower myself to you as you take me back, as you mark me as yours. I'm not a submissive wolf, Jason. I'm a fucking strong dominant, and all I want is to show the world that you are mine and mark you as mine. I want to wear your mark so no other man can think he can just take me because he wants to prove how dominant he is. I want to sink my fangs into you as you sink your cock into me. That is what I want. That is what my wolf is craving, and that is what I can't have."

I swallowed hard, images of exactly what she was painting slamming into my mind with such veracity I nearly shook.

"Dear God," I whispered, and a small smile played on her face, her cheeks blushing a slight pink.

"I'm not usually that open when I say those things. They just tumbled out of me. I don't know how to deal with it, and I don't know what we're going to do, but I'm here for Spencer. Do you understand that?"

I swallowed hard. "Because he was your Packmate, not your mate?" I asked, wondering what I would look like without a throat if she tore it out at that question.

"I'm going to let that slide because I know you are feeling the mating urge as a human, even as I feel it as a wolf. No, Spencer wasn't mine. He lost his potential, what you are to me in this exact moment, during the wars."

Grief settled into me, a heavy coat right along my skin. "I'm so sorry."

"We lost a lot of people in our wars. A lot of wolves, a lot of potentials that would never come to fruition."

"And you're saying this potential can fade away and not become anything beyond what it is right now?" I asked, wondering if I wanted the answer.

"I'm not saying that," she stated, and winced. "More that I don't know what we need or what I want, but we need to focus on the here and now. I wasn't expecting this, Jason. You're human. You must never have expected this."

"No, not this."

This urge was overwhelming, and I felt as if I could barely breathe or hold on to or do anything other than wanting the woman, the wolf, the beauty in front of me.

"You are strength personified, Kaylee. It's hard to focus when you're around, especially considering we met with you throwing me on my back."

She threw her head back and laughed at that, the tension easing out of the room even as it ramped in a new direction.

"I'm not going to apologize for that."

"I didn't ask you to."

"I don't know what's going to happen or what we're going to do about it, but do you understand that I need to do my duty? I was so close to finding Spencer, and I lost him. My Pack needed him, and I wasn't able to protect him."

"It wasn't your fault."

"Tell me that once we find the murderers."

"I can do that. Because we're going to."

"After that, though, after that, you and I can talk, and we can figure out exactly what this whole mating thing means."

"After," I whispered, knowing that was the right decision. It was hard enough to think when she was around. If we touched any more than we already had, I'd be lost. And I think we both knew that.

"So we do our best not to have a repeat."

"Not until we find Spencer's killers."

I would say that would give more incentive, but I already had enough, wanting to find the creatures or men or whoever they are who were doing this to our people.

Our. Because they were humans, witches, wolves. All species, all who wanted a life, a dream of a future, and had been snuffed out for whatever reason. I wanted to find out that reason. I wanted to take away the guilt on Kaylee's face. A guilt she shouldn't feel.

"I have my papers here, but do you want to go back to the den? That way we're surrounded by others and not alone in my tiny apartment?"

I hadn't meant to ask like that, but when Kaylee grinned, her shoulders eased ever so slightly.

"That would be amazing. Because it's tough to think when it's just the two of us."

"I want to take that as a compliment, but if I do, then I'm going to have to tell you it feels the same when I'm alone with you...and when we're surrounded by others."

"Oh."

"You say potential. Does that mean we could walk away from this?"

Why did it hurt? Why did it feel like whatever the answer was, if it wasn't right, something I never knew I wanted would break me?

"A potential does mean you can walk away, but I've only heard of two or three people in my entire life who've ever done it. Sometimes you can find more than one mate in the centuries that a shifter can live. Sometimes it takes a century to find that person.

"And so that means I'm it. We're it."

"If it works. The Moon Goddess has given us a choice, but sometimes she seems to know what she's talking about."

"You don't have to sound so resigned, Kaylee," I said dryly. However, I didn't feel affronted at all. I wasn't part of this world. I lived on the periphery. And yet, it seemed I was being thrown right into it.

"It depends on the person. The situation."

"Would I have to be a wolf?" I asked, confused.

She winced. "I think so. Sometimes you don't. My dad isn't. But he has his own magic."

"Really?"

"My dad is a tracker like me, but his is with magic. My mom is a witch."

"And yet you're part of the Pack? And a wolf?" I was a little confused as to the genetics at play here.

"My father is a wolf, and even though genetically he's not mine, the Moon Goddess made it easy, so all three of my parents' genetics somehow mixed in with us. I'm not quite sure how it happened, but all of my siblings and I are wolves, even if Josh, my dad, is biologically my father. Some of us took tracking traits, some of us took witch's traits. It's all very complicated, but it happens with the triad bond."

"You're going to need to sit down with me and go over all of this." I grinned, my brain going a mile a minute. "I'm a geneticist, after all."

Her eyes widened. "For some reason I had forgotten that when talking about this."

"Magic and genetics? I didn't know they mixed."

"Sometimes, they seem to cancel one another out. Hence my family."

"It's all fascinating. And I'm going to have to know everything." I paused. "Everything," I stressed.

"Jason. It's so complicated. For our mating bond to work, for you to live as long as our mating bond breathes life—my lifetime—you'd have to turn to wolf. Do you understand that? It's painful, and the only way that our laws allow it is for a mating."

"Your laws or the laws of the United States?" I asked.

"The laws of the humans that were put upon us once they found out we were alive. Wolf laws have always been slightly different, though no one ever went out to create wolves unless they were creating an army to take over another Pack, and that was a whole other thing."

"I want to know it all, Kaylee. I need to know it all."

"Okay. I can do that. But first, we need to find out what happened to Spencer. To the others. And that means going back to the den because it's tough to be alone in the same room with you."

I groaned, my dick growing harder, if that was even possible. "You're making this difficult."

"You're standing there with a steel rod in your pants. Let's talk about being difficult, shall we?" she teased and turned to walk out of the room. I picked up my bag and followed her, and did my best not to look at her ass as she moved.

She was gorgeous, and she could be mine. How the hell had that happened?

"So, we head back to the den, maybe work with the others to try to find answers."

"We can do that. And then after?"

"Then after."

We stepped outside, headed towards my car, when she froze, her gaze going on alert.

"By any chance, do you know how to fight?" she whispered, and I stiffened, my hand going to the blade in my bag.

"A little. Riaz wanted to make sure I knew what I was doing with a weapon."

"Good, because you're going to need it."

# CHAPTER 12

Jason

MY WHOLE BODY stiffened impossibly as men in black garb, their faces hidden and weapons in their hands, prowled towards us.

I blinked. I had been expecting wolves or something else paranormal, and perhaps they were, but they weren't in wolf form.

No, they had weapons.

And from the look of those tranq guns in their hands, as well as the knives and other instruments strapped to their bodies, they weren't playing around.

"Damn it," Kaylee whispered, and then there wasn't much time to think.

I shuffled to the side, ducking out of the way of one of the men with the knives.

Nobody was shooting. Instead, it looked like they wanted to subdue us, for us to fight back, so they could stab or do something else to us. I wasn't sure what it was, but nobody was using their guns.

The man with the knife closest to me slashed at my chest, and I ducked out of the way, pulling out my own weapon to fight.

"Jason, watch out!" Kaylee shouted, and I ducked as a man with a lead pipe came at me. Knives, lead pipes, and the guns holstered?

Something was off. Did these men want to hurt us? Kill us? Or take us?

Chills broke out over my body as I thought about it. These were, what, some form of commandos that were coming after us? Did it have to do with the black marks? Or maybe this is something completely different. I didn't know. Only one guy was coming after me. The other four were going after Kaylee.

Fuck. This team knew Kaylee was a wolf. They knew that she was the aggressive one.

I may know how to fight because Riaz wanted to make sure I knew what I was doing, but I wasn't the strong one in this situation. I wasn't going to be the one that could protect her.

I could try, but my brain is what got me through. I wasn't a wolf. I didn't have the skills to protect her, but I could do my best not to be a liability. That would be how I protected her. And myself. I wouldn't force her attention on me while I acted like an idiot trying to protect the woman that could really protect herself and everyone else around her.

"Get her. She's who the boss wants."

Kaylee's gaze met my own, her eyes glowing gold with the wolf as claws slid out of her fingertips.

She was glorious, a fighter, and they wanted her.

I'd be damned if I let them get her.

I pulled up my arm, my blade in my hand, as the other man came down with a knife towards me, his blade hitting mine with a metal clang. I cursed, the sharp sting of metal against flesh, the flesh of my forearm searing.

Kaylee's nostrils flared as she glared over at us.

"Don't die, Jason. I'm not done with you yet."

I would have smiled at that, would have pounded my chest, or at least puffed up a bit, but I didn't have time.

Riaz may have taught me how to fight with the blade, but the main thing he had taught me was to run.

To get out of there so those who knew how to fight could protect me. If I was ever in the den during the attack, my job was to stay near the children and help them. To get them to safety, along with the maternal wolves. I might not be a submissive wolf, but I was a human. And I was a scientist. I had no idea how the hell I had gotten here, but I knew this had to have something to do with whatever was leaving those black bite marks all over people. What was killing people.

With who had killed the Redwood wolf, Kaylee's friend, Spencer.

"I see that they have the human pet," the man in front of me snarled as the other four men fought Kaylee. She fought back, but they were all strong, far stronger than I thought they should be for humans. Maybe they were wolves or witches. I didn't know. I didn't know enough about this world, now I was surrounded by it, not able to do anything but try to protect myself so Kaylee could do what she needed to. There had to be other wolves around, someone to see this, and yet nobody was coming. Yes, we were in the forested area, hidden off to the side, but there had to be others.

"I'm not a pet," I snarled, finally answering the man in front of me.

"You're a human fighting with those animals. Maybe they're the pets, and you're just their owner? No, looks like the little lady over there is the one that does all the fighting. What do you do? Nothing, except get in our way, Dr. Jason Torres."

My eyes narrowed. "Excuse me?"

He knew who I was. And that I was a doctor. What the hell was going on? Had I gotten close to figuring out what was going on? Or was I just being paranoid?

"You got a little too close, Jason, but I guess you would've known that. But don't worry, we'll make sure your little wolf knows exactly what's coming to her when we do it."

I growled, the insinuation of what exactly he had just said hit me hard, and I lashed out, slicing the man against the forearm. "Don't you dare touch her."

"You think you can protect the little wolf? You're nothing. Just a human."

"And you're not?" I asked, focusing in on what he said.

"You don't know what I am. I'm not weak like you. Soon, the world will know exactly who we are. And exactly why you can't be around to tell people what you found."

I knew it was too late. As soon as he finished those words, Kaylee cried out, but she wasn't the one bleeding.

I let out a huff of breath as I lurched forward,

throwing my knife towards the man. It was all I could do, after all.

He twisted his blade into my guts, the cool knife sliding into my skin like warm butter. What an odd thing to think.

I was dying. This had to be death.

I fell to my knees, my hands going to the wound at my side. I tried to breathe, I tried to do anything, yet there was nothing. Rocks stuck into my knees as I fell, and I looked up at the man in front of me, a smile on his face.

"Too late, too close, too much of nothing," he snarled. Blood pooled down my chin, and I cursed and then held my blade up before throwing it directly at the man. His eyes widened as if he couldn't believe what he was seeing. My knife buried into his neck and he screamed, blood spurting. Kaylee screamed. My hand went back to the wound at my side, trying to hold my stomach together, but I couldn't.

Couldn't do anything.

Why didn't it hurt? Why wasn't there any more searing pain?

I could feel my heartbeat in my gut wound, and I knew that probably wasn't a good thing.

Only, I couldn't care. Couldn't think. Everything was so slow, and I had to wonder what was going on.

Kaylee yelled again, and then she lashed out to get to me, and the four men were down on the ground, their throats slit as her body flew forward, shaking with rage.

I found myself with my head on her thigh, looking up at her, wondering exactly how I had got gotten here.

There were footsteps, shouts, but I couldn't hear any of them. I could only see Kaylee's face as she screamed.

And then there was nothing.

# CHAPTER 13

Kaylee

THIS COULDN'T BE HAPPENING. Jason couldn't be dead.

My voice echoed throughout the forest as others came towards us, Riaz running full tilt, shirtless, no shoes, and looking as if he had just thrown sweats over his body as he ran, his entire body radiating that of Alpha.

"Where were you?" I shouted, my throat raw. "Where were you? Why weren't you here? Why wasn't anyone here?"

Brendan and Dean fell to my side along with Riaz,

as other wolves surrounded the area, checking on the bodies that lay strewn around us, as well as anyone else that was near.

"There is magic coming," Dean whispered, and my gaze went to his, then towards Riaz's bright gold ones.

"Magic? With those witches?"

"They all look human, but they smell off," Brendan snarled. "Like they came into contact with something I don't recognize."

"I don't understand what's going on," I gasped, trying to feel for a pulse. "Is he dead? Is Jason dead?" I screamed.

"I can still feel him there, damn it, we're losing him. And I don't know what's going on either. It was as if there was a magical barrier, a ward all on its own keeping you from us. That's why we weren't here. That's why we didn't come in time. We should have been here faster. We aren't that far from the apartments."

"Jason?" I whispered, looking down at him. His eyes were closed, his mouth parted, and I couldn't feel him. Why couldn't I feel him? This was my mate. He was supposed to be here,

"Kaylee," Riaz snapped, and I looked up at him, my wolf bristling, wanting to lash out, wanting to do anything, but this was an Alpha, maybe not my Alpha, but he could kill me with one blink.

"What do we do?" I asked, feeling as if I was losing myself. Losing everything.

"We can turn him. There's still time."

In order to turn a human into a wolf, they had to be near death. It wasn't with a single bite, and suddenly you would shift at the blue moon and live a happy little life in the supernatural. That's not how real life works.

You had to be dead, with the saliva of a wolf's bite over the majority of your body, as well as claw marks, with a brutality that meant that you were turning into a new part of yourself, joining a world that wasn't one like you had come from.

I remember hearing the horror stories of how some of my aunts and uncles had been turned into wolves once they had mated into the Pack and needed to become something other than human for the mating bond to fully complete.

Others of my family and Pack had nearly been dead, and marking them, creating a mating bond is what had saved them.

Then it all clicked for me, and I knew why Riaz was saying it.

"If you turn him right now and someone finds out, they'll kill Jason. Maybe even you."

Because at the moment, unless it was for a mating, you could not save another person. You could not turn them. Because we were at the precipice of a new era in shifter politics, and right now, the humans were winning. Not for long, I had to hope, but for now, even if we saved Jason, he could still die if anybody found out he was turned.

And with the way things were going these days, they would find out.

"Mark him. Bite him. Try to turn him."

"Kaylee. Is he yours? Is what I saw real?" I looked up at him then, my whole body shaking.

"He is my potential. He could be mine."

The Starlight Pack Healer was near, kneeling by us, trying to stop the bleeding, and it was slowing, but only because Jason's heart was slowing.

He was dying, and I couldn't feel anything. I couldn't keep up.

"Kaylee. If he's yours, mark him."

"You know that's not how you complete the bond."

"He'll be mated, he'll have a mate, and you can complete the bond later. It will give me the authority to change him. I don't know if you are Alpha enough to do it. If you're dominant enough. But I am."

Riaz touched my face, and I snarled at him. He held his hand up, brows raised. The other wolves growled toward me, the balance of power standing on the tip of a blade. I had just tried to bite their Alpha, and I didn't blame them. But nobody was going to touch me just then, not without fear of getting something bitten off.

"Kaylee. I don't know if you're dominant enough to have the power and the strength in your wolf in order to change him. I'm not saying you are weak. I'm saying I need to do this." He looked at his Healer. "I'm right, right? It's the only way?"

The Healer gave me a sad look. "I'm sorry. There's nothing I can do. I don't think a human doctor could do anything either."

My wolf howled, and I whimpered, looking down at Jason's pale face, his skin nearly gray.

"Okay. Okay. I have to do something." I started shaking as I pulled him closer, my fangs elongating. "I don't want him to die. He can't die."

"Then do it. We don't have a lot of time."

Riaz stood up and pulled off his pants, and I didn't bother to look. He needed to shift, to be in wolf form for this.

I didn't, though, not for this part.

"I'm sorry," I whispered.

Tears slid down my cheeks as I bit at his neck, marking him as mine. My wolf howled in sorrowed triumph, anguished joy.

Because this was our mate, I was marking him as mine.

This mark would fade, though, and the wound would heal, but what it meant would be forever. It would be lasting.

The first part of the meeting bond snapped into place, no longer a potential, but half of a whole.

Soon we would have to complete the mating bond by having sex, by marking each other in the ways of wolves and shifters, but for now, this was the first step, the first step into a forever with a man I didn't know.

He had fought with bravery and tried to protect me without getting in my way.

He had done so much, but it wasn't enough.

I hadn't been enough for him.

I looked up as Riaz came forward, having shifted into a wolf. He couldn't shift as quickly as Connor could, but he was dominant enough that he had done it fast. And had probably forced him to change into his wolf far faster than he normally would in order to protect Jason.

I would thank him for that later.

But for now, I couldn't.

I couldn't do anything.

Dean pulled me back, holding me, and I snarled and

snapped at him, angry for taking me away from my mate.

"Stop it. I can do this."

"You don't need to see this," he whispered, and I pulled away from him, but Brendan was there, holding me back.

"No. You know this is going to be too much for you to see."

"I won't leave him alone. Not with everything that's happening."

So we stood there, as the men held me back, taking my beatings as I thrashed and I bit and my wolf pushed at me, sending me nearly over the edge, closer than I have ever been in my life as I struggled against their restraints.

Because Riaz was hurting my mate.

Riaz's claws dug into his flesh, his fangs puncturing Jason's body. Jason was out of it, would feel no pain, wouldn't be part of this.

I was grateful for that, because the drugs to knock somebody out negated part of the magic, not so the changing wouldn't work, but intensified the pain.

So the fact that Jason was been near death had been a blessing because he wouldn't feel this, not like others.

I felt it.

Every mark, every bite, every rending of flesh.

I felt it on my own body.

My wolf snarled and growled and howled. She didn't want this for her mate, didn't want this to happen.

Tears slid from my eyes as I choked sobs, wanting my mate, wanting my family, wanting anything but these two near strangers holding me back from taking care of my mate.

Then the Healer was there, a strange expression on her face as she went to heal Jason's wounds.

Because Jason would be a wolf at the next full moon. He wouldn't need full moons to change, but the one after the transformation was strengthened by the moon itself.

Somebody had come here, had tried to kill me, had nearly succeeded in killing Jason.

And now our lives would be irrevocably tangled, and Jason had just lost his humanity.

"I took his choice," I whispered, my voice raw, so ravaged that I could barely breathe.

Riaz, having shifted to human, held me as Dean handed me a bottle of water. Brendan moved to help the Healer as Rio paced around the group of us.

"It was the only choice."

"Was it?" I asked, but nobody answered, because they couldn't.

Jason had not had the ability to speak up. Maybe he would have wanted to die rather than become a wolf.

Maybe he would have rather ended his life in that moment, not come back at all, than become my mate.

And now we would never know.

He was my mate, and he would be a wolf.

And Jason had never had a choice.

I would always be the one who took that choice from him.

One hell of a way to begin a mating.

# CHAPTER 14

Kaylee

I DIDN'T REMEMBER GETTING BACK to the den. The others had moved around the fight site, looking over the bodies. Not Jason's. No, the Healer, Brendan, and Riaz had taken Jason back to the den to take care of him, to make sure he was settled before he woke up.

I would go to him soon, I would hold his hand, and I would wait for him to wake. And I would wait for the recrimination in his eyes as he realized that I had taken so much from him.

I didn't want to hate myself for doing that. I didn't want to hate the person that I was becoming. But I had taken so much from him. He would no longer be human. He would no longer have any sense of who he was, because I had been the one to decide that.

I hadn't wanted him to die.

I had wanted my mate.

I had come down to Texas to find Spencer, to find my Packmate and see if he had become a rogue or if he had just been out of communication.

I hadn't expected to find Spencer's dead body as I had. I hadn't expected to find him wrapped up in the mystery of strange humans that seemed to have far more strength than they should.

And I sure as hell hadn't meant to find Jason.

Now that I had, I wasn't sure what I was supposed to do.

Jason had nearly died. And Spencer was dead. And now I was mated to Jason, at least partially, and there was no going back from that.

Once my mate woke up and realized what I had done, I had to hope he wouldn't walk away, that he wouldn't leave our wolves half broken, half mated.

I kissed him, and he had kissed me back, and we had nearly taken each other against his door, and yet that was the closest we had gotten to talking about anything of who we were.

What was I supposed to do with that?

My head shot up at the feeling of a familiar wolf. I nearly ran across the field where I had been standing outside of the building Riaz had brought Jason to.

My father Reed stood at the other end of the field, my cousin Parker with him, and I ran towards them, not caring who saw me.

I didn't have to growl and raise my chin and my fist to be strong.

We were wolves. We were Pack animals.

And my Pack had come.

I threw my arms around my father, holding him close as Reed kissed the top of my head before I turned to Parker. The Voice of the Wolves, my cousin, the wolf that had brought the Redwood Pack and the Starlight Pack together in the first place, held me close.

"How are you here?" I asked, my throat aching.

Parker frowned at me and then gave me his bottle of water. "Drink. Tell us what's going on."

"You first. Why are you here?" I asked, even though I did gulp down some of the water.

"We came for Spencer," my father whispered as he kissed the top of my head. My wolf whimpered, and I leaned into them both, wondering how I could have forgotten that.

Then again, I didn't know the plan with everybody

else. For all I knew they could have sent anybody—even the Alpha at this point.

I hadn't been thinking. Not since I had seen Jason. And that was the problem. I couldn't keep up with my thoughts, but here I was, partially mated, and there was no going back from that.

"I smell a human yet not human on you," my father said, and I blushed as Parker let out a breath.

"That was very subtle, Uncle Reed."

"There's nothing subtle about me, and we all know it."

I wasn't sure if that was the case, but as I let them hold me, aware others were watching, I didn't cry. They had seen me cry before, saw the sobs rack my body as I tried to keep up with my emotions. They didn't need to see anything else.

"We need to meet with the Alpha," Parker said after a moment. "And then why don't you tell us what's going on?"

I nodded, rolled my shoulders back. I was the Tracker of the Redwood Pack. I needed to be stronger than this. And I needed to not confuse my family and terrify them along the way.

"I'll introduce you to Riaz," I said to my father, before I looked at Parker. "Though you've met him."

"You seem to have a form of connection," Parker said, brow raised.

"Not in the way you think."

My father's eyes narrowed. "Talk to us."

"I found my mate."

My father's eyes widened as Parker grinned.

"Really? Is it Riaz?"

I snorted. "No, not Riaz. My mate...he is...was, a human."

"*Was?*" my father asked, blinking. "Talk to us as we walk."

"Maybe we should do this with Riaz, because I don't know what they know at this point. Everything's moved so quickly."

"Come on," Parker said as he gripped my hand. "Let's go."

We didn't need to go far, as Riaz met us halfway there, and we stepped into the building where Jason was sleeping in another room. I wanted to go there, and I would. I needed to explain to my family and Riaz what had been going on so that I could lead them all to talk about what they needed to, and I could focus on Jason.

Then I would rip out the throats of anybody that came near my mate again. I would avenge the loss of his human-ity, because even if Jason hated me for the rest of his life for what I had done, I would kill anybody that came near him. Because that's who I was, I was a dominant wolf. I was a Redwood wolf. And they would have to deal with it.

I was a Redwood wolf, wasn't I? It broke my heart, reaching out towards the bonds of my family and my other wolves, and I knew that was the truth.

I was Redwood. Was Jason Starlight? I wasn't sure. I had never really known of a mating like ours, not while crossing Pack lines. Matings with the Redwoods and Talons, and even the Aspens now, were completely different.

I didn't know, and we would have to work on it soon to figure it out. But for now, I focused on what I could— my family.

"Why don't you tell us what's going on?" my father said.

"Your daughter is a strong wolf, and while I know she would be an advantage for our Pack, I'm glad to see she is with our future ally," Riaz said out of the blue, and I looked between him and Parker, but Parker just grinned as Reed glared a bit, and shook his head.

"Start at the beginning, daughter of mine. I don't like to be confused."

I knew he was playing the part of the old man to settle me, and it was working. The sense of familiar and home soothed my wolf. "Okay, I can try."

I tried to explain about finding Spencer and Jason, about the bite marks and the random rogues that might not be rogues, and the mutant bites that didn't make any sense. I explained about the commandos that we had met.

And the fact that Jason, a human geneticist that was the friend of the Starlight Pack, was my mate.

And we were only partially mated.

Reed let out a little soft growl before he reached forward and hugged me tightly. "I'm so sorry, daughter of mine. That must've been a horrible decision."

"He's still not awake, Father. I don't know what I'm supposed to do."

"You will go be by his side, and you will hold his hand. When the time comes, you will talk to him about what happened. He will understand. He is your mate."

"But I forced it."

"The Moon Goddess doesn't make a mistake like that," Parker replied, and I looked at Parker, and then my father, and I had to wonder if maybe that was true. After all, both of them were in triads, both of them found not one, but two mates, and somehow were making it work. Both sets of matings had been under traumatic and dangerous circumstances, maybe I could do the same. But I didn't know.

"So you don't know who these soldiers were?" Reed

asked, and Riaz shook his head.

"No. Not yet. We have their bodies. We're going to find out who they are."

I let out a breath, my wolf pacing, both of us wanted to go to Jason. "I'm sorry I didn't leave one alive."

"Considering they had just stuck a knife into Jason's stomach, I understand. Between the use of the magic to keep the other wolves away from what was going on and the fact that they also had darts with some kind of serum in it? I'm fine. I understand. We'll figure it out. Jason will wake up. He will be Pack. We'll figure it out."

"He'll be Redwood Pack," Parker said, and I blinked, wondering why Parker was so adamant.

"Of course he will, Voice of the Wolves. You don't need to be dry with me. However, it will make some new ties with the Starlight Pack."

"So you're saying that he'll be Redwood Pack, and the Starlight Pack is just going to let him go, free and easy? Or are you just saying that because you don't think he'll even choose that? Because I took this choice from him."

"Kaylee," Reed whispered, but it was Riaz who spoke next.

"I'm saying that because I have to believe in the Moon Goddess, just like the rest of you. Our Pack doesn't have as many fated mates as others. We're secrets of our own," he said, and I knew the fact that he had said any of that at all was a large calculation and a step towards trust between the two Packs. From the way that my father and Parker looked at one another, they understood that too.

"Jason will understand. There were reasons that we never brought him into our Pack, not just because of the rules of our new world. But because something held us back."

"You mean so that he could nearly die as a human on the battlefield?"

Riaz cursed under his breath. "No. Because he needed to be with you. Your Pack. And another connection for us to one of the strongest Packs in the world while we struggle to find a new footing in this unhinged version of it, that's something that I feel like the Moon Goddess is preparing us for."

"But first, we need Jason to wake up."

"And then we need to figure out who the hell is killing our people," Riaz growled.

The four of us spoke some more before Brendan, Rio, and Dean walked in and joined the conversation. We tried to figure out exactly who had come at us and were waiting to see what kind of serum was in those darts, only to find out that it had been a simple tranquilizer for wolves.

Someone knew our biology enough to try to attack us, but with so many of our secrets out in the open, that wasn't as unheard of as it had been even ten years ago.

Somebody was hunting wolves, and with the way that those humans had smelled wrong and the magic involved in those fake wards, I had to believe it was somehow connected to these black bite marks.

We were missing something, something big, and I had to wonder exactly what it was.

The Healer came out after a moment, saying I could sit with Jason, and so I left my family with the others, knowing that they could take care of themselves, and I went to Jason's room.

He had said he had no family, that the Pack were the only friends he had, and now he was lying here on the bed, alone, possibly never to awake. Possibly to hate me once he did.

I let out a shaky breath, my wolf whimpering, as I took his hand.

"I'm sorry. I'm sorry for making your choice. Don't hate me."

I let out a breath and gasped as Jason opened his eyes.

"Kaylee."

And I was lost.

# CHAPTER 15

Jason

I COULD FEEL something prowl within me. Something that wasn't me, or perhaps had never been there before. How did I know what this feeling was? And how did I know that this was always meant to be?

I shook my head as I gripped the edge of the bathroom sink. I looked into the mirror, sweat coating my brow, and let out a deep breath. Only it came out more of a rumble, and I froze, wondering what that was, who that could be.

I wiped the steam from the window, my shower having been hot enough to scorch the skin off my bones.

Not that I wouldn't have been able to possibly heal from that since, apparently, I was now a shifter. A wolf. A werewolf to some, a monster to others.

A mate to Kaylee.

How had this happened? Oh, I knew *how* it had happened. Someone had stabbed me in the guts, men in black garb with knives and tranq guns. They had killed me. I had felt that.

As a scientist, as one who needed answers and not just facsimiles of what could be and couldn't be, I had always known I would die. I hadn't known when, or how. But I had known that one day I would be at the end of my line. That death would take me. Yet, it hadn't this time. Somehow, without Kaylee and I doing more than kissing against that door, a bare brush of need, our mating bond had taken. We had skipped a few of the steps, if what I knew about wolves was true. But she had marked me.

My hand went up to my shoulder, my fingertips brushing along the ridges. The only scar I had left on my body. And Kaylee had whispered to me when she had thought I had still been sleeping that this scar would fade. That mates sometimes would mark each other again, over and over, in a sign of deep pleasure. Possession.

What if we both wanted this? Wanted more? I had heard the temperance in her tone, the hesitation.

She was afraid.

Afraid that she had taken my choice.

Then again, what was a choice?

I was a wolf. Someone had tried to kill me. I had a mate.

I was Pack.

My life was irrevocably altered, the path laid out before me something I had never once thought could ever be, and here I was, wondering at the idea of what life and death were.

Because I had died, but then I hadn't.

I had been slain, and then I had risen.

I rubbed my temples, a small smile appointing on my face.

Did sharing a soul with a wolf make one go insane? Or begin to go down the idea of spirituality and what a person could be?

As I had thought before, I had known that I would die one day, but now as a wolf that day could be centuries in the future.

Some of the wolves I knew within the Starlight Pack were hundreds of years old. The elders have seen wars and the creation of a country, of a civilization.

And here I was, possibly looking into a future that I hadn't planned.

Or maybe it always would have been mine. I was a friend of the Pack, after all. And though finding a mate seemed far out of the question, there were ways to become Pack without breaking the newly instated law that the government had on how to become a wolf shifter in these lands.

There was a knock on the door, pulling me from my thoughts, and I cleared my throat, sensing who it was.

I frowned, *sensing?* I inhaled and was nearly assaulted by a thousand different scents that were too much for me. I sneezed, let out a growl, an actual growl, and slapped my hand over my mouth.

"Jason? I'm coming in."

Kaylee walked in, opening the door, her eyes wide as she stared at me, my body practically radiating with tension as I had one hand over my mouth, eyes wide.

She blinked at me, a small smile playing on her face.

"I just heard you growl. Are you okay?" She reached forward, put her hand on my chest before she pulled back as if the touch had singed both of us.

"Sorry, I didn't mean to touch you without asking. Damn it. You okay?"

Her wolf was in her gaze then, I could see the gold. And my eyes felt different, everything was in slightly sharper focus as if I could see things I hadn't before.

I blinked and realized that I didn't need my contacts. I didn't need anything.

I could see.

"I'm fine," I sighed as I lowered my hand. "I feel like an idiot, though. I'm getting used to all these new senses. I can see."

"And I bet you can smell more, hear more, and it's going to be a lot all at once. When you're ready to shift and the moon pulls you, it's going to get even harder, but we'll be there for you. We'll help you learn how to deal with this new body of yours and what it means to share a body with a wolf."

I swallowed hard. "So, there's another soul inside me?"

Warmth infused me, was it my wolf? Yes, my wolf began to pace within me, and I could almost visualize it as he moved within me, getting to know his new surroundings just like I was getting to know him being there.

Kaylee smiled softly and held out her hand. "First, let's get you a shirt, because I'm going to be honest, it's tough to think with you shirtless."

I blinked. "Really? I mean, come on, I know I look okay, but okay."

Kaylee snorted. "We're mates. I think you're hot. I think you knew that. And, well, I'm usually pretty blunt. I don't hide my feelings, even though sometimes I feel that I need to. I know we have a lot to talk about, with what happened out there on the fields, not just with the attack, but with what happened after. We also need to talk about whatever serum that they're using or whatever's going on. But first, come up. Let's get that shirt on you so I can see. And then I'm here to answer your questions, I promise."

"I want to kiss you right now." I hadn't even realized that the words were coming until I blurted them, and she smiled softly.

"Good. Because I want to kiss you too. However, the Starlight Pack is waiting to meet you."

I froze, confused, and oddly wary. "They know me."

And Kaylee was Redwood. Would that mean we would be different Packs? No, that wasn't right. Why the hell couldn't I focus? Everything was just too much all at once.

"They want to meet your wolf. Don't worry. We all want to make sure that you're going through this as smoothly as possible, considering the circumstances. Now, what did I say about your shirt?"

My lips quirked into a smile, and I moved past her, my hip brushing against hers. We both froze, and I swallowed hard, my legs practically going weak. I could smell her, that scent. That was what I had scented through the door.

It was Kaylee. Mine, all mine.

Only...not yet? Maybe not yet. Because we hadn't slept together, and didn't you need to do that in order to have a mate?

I had so many questions, and I knew Kaylee had answers, but it was tough to focus.

Someone knocked on the door, and Kaylee's hackles rose before she moved past me, pointed at the shirt, and I slid it over my shoulders. She nodded tightly, then opened the door. My gaze went to Riaz's instinctually, and then I lowered my eyes, just as instinctually.

Riaz let out a grumble, moved past Kaylee, who growled softly, but Riaz just quirked his lips.

"You're awake. Good. And showered. I know that you two need some time alone, but your wolf needs to know where he stands."

"He's Redwood, Riaz. You know that."

I looked at Kaylee, meeting her gaze. Was she more dominant than me? How the hell was I supposed to know who was dominant? Was I going to have to do challenges in order to figure that out?

"Dominance challenges take time, and yes, you will have to do dominance challenges."

I looked up at Riaz. "Did I say all of that out loud?"

"You did," Kaylee said with a smile. "And no, you're not more dominant than me, but you're my mate, so you can meet my gaze. Meeting Riaz's is harder, and once you get to know your wolf, especially after the first shift, your dominance can change. That can always change, depending on who you are. I don't think you're going to be a submissive wolf, nor do I think you're going to be middle of the Pack. I can feel it here." She put her hand over her chest. "However, we're going to need to take our time with that. And you are Redwood."

"So, I'm not yours then?" I asked Riaz, before I looked over back at Kaylee.

"You're not. But I'm the closest Alpha around right now because we are in a unique situation, so my wolf is here to keep you in line before your first shift."

"What does that mean?" I asked, my eyes wide.

"That means your wolf is going to take a little bit of time for you to gain control of it. It can be dangerous, especially when you haven't shifted yet."

"Dangerous for me, or for others?" I asked, full of worry.

"Either," Kaylee said. "But you're going to be fine. I'm going to be here. Now, come on. Let's talk."

"You know those words are never good when they come from a woman," I mumbled, and Riaz laughed.

"They're from your mate, so they're really not good."

"Oh, good. We're going to play boy-games. I can't wait." She said dryly.

"Okay, I have questions."

"And maybe we have answers," Riaz said as he moved towards the couch in the small living room.

We were in one of the small homes that Riaz and the Pack built on Pack grounds for guests. They weren't the same buildings that were outside of the den wards where Kaylee had stayed. It seemed they wanted to keep me safe, even though I wasn't Pack.

I still wasn't sure exactly what was going on, but I was learning.

At least, I hoped so.

"So, I'm a werewolf."

"Or a shifter. We pretty much go by shifters. Although you can use werewolf."

"I won't offend anybody if I do?" I asked.

Riaz shook his head. "No, though werewolves are more in the movies. The ones that shift into half human, half wolf, and terrorize the night."

"So you don't have like a warrior form then?"

Kaylee frowned and looked over at Riaz. "I thought you said that he was a friend of the Pack. Shouldn't he already know these things?"

"I'm right here," I teased.

"What? You're sitting here thinking about warrior forms."

"Our warrior form is if we can use our claws or our fangs while in human form, but we don't get a hunchback and howl at the moon."

"Unless I hear my brother when he's drunk. But we don't like to talk about that," Kaylee teased, her eyes dancing. Her wolf was in her eyes again. I really wanted to meet her wolf. Damn it. I wanted to meet mine too.

Even though everything had come from near tragedy, I was excited.

"I can feel your wolf's excitement, but let me stop you here. Any genetics studies that you complete do not go to the government, you get me?" Riaz asked, and I blinked. "Of course not. I would never betray you guys. Even before, well, all of this."

"You want to bleed a little bit just to study what's going on inside you?" Kaylee asked, tilting her head in the way of the wolf.

"I like the science behind things."

"And the Moon Goddess is the magic behind it," Kaylee began. "Long ago, a hunter killed for sport, not for protection and not to feed his family. The Moon Goddess was in such pain from seeing such a thing. She saved the dying wolf's soul by placing it inside the hunter's body so he could feel what he had done."

I swallowed hard, remembering some of the stories, but hearing it from Kaylee's lips felt as if we were in some form of ceremony.

She continued. "When the hunter came back to his family, he shifted. Eventually, he bit others, either in combat or in just the way of his wolf. The first three have a long, convoluted reincarnation story with some of the Talons," Kaylee added, her eyes dancing.

Riaz grinned. "It's true then? The stories"

"Maybe. Or maybe I'm just pulling your tail."

"I'm going to have to get up and meet some of these Talons."

"The first Pack from this wolf later became a well-known Pack of ours. However, all this is to say that our wolves are family based, are bond-oriented. The Alpha rules, but he cares. He's the one that protects everybody. At all times. The Heir is next in line, and shares some of the mantle."

Riaz added. "The Beta protects the Pack from within while the Enforcer protects the Pack from outside forces."

Kaylee nodded. "While the Omega heals the soul and the Healer heals the body."

"I know all of this. And there are Trackers, an Enforcer, and lieutenants, and there are other magics within the Packs as well. Some I don't know."

"A lot of Pack magic is held close to the vest. I might know the Redwood secrets, but I may never know all the Talon secrets, even if we're nearly one Pack at this point."

"And don't even get me started on mine," Riaz added with a wink, and I shook my head, wondering why Riaz was so open with me, even if I wasn't a Starlight member.

"Everything that we're telling you here is in the open. These aren't our secrets."

"Nor was the urban legend you seem to think of the three of the Talon Pack that I mentioned," Kaylee added with a snort. "You are wolf. Not born, but made. Shifting will be difficult, and I know it's going to be painful, and I'm so sorry that this happened. I'm sorry that your choice was taken from you and that I had to be the one to do it."

"I did it too," Riaz added. He met my gaze, and I wanted to reach out and pull Kaylee closer to tell her that she was fine, that she did it for a reason, and I didn't hate her. But I felt as if we should be alone for that. This was a far too personal thing to be speaking of with Riaz.

"I'm the one that changed you. You needed a dominant wolf, one even more dominant than Kaylee, even though she's close." He pulled his gaze from me and looked over at Kaylee. "Another five, ten years, Kaylee?

You'll have the strength to do that. I can feel your wolf."

She rolled her shoulders back, raising her chin. "Good to know. I just wish I could have done something more."

"Kaylee, the bond kept him here." Riaz looked over at me again, and I nodded.

"I knew I was dying, but I felt something click within me, and I stayed."

Kaylee leaned forward, a tear running down her cheek. I cursed under my breath, moved forward to brush it away from her skin.

"Don't cry. I'm okay."

Riaz cleared his throat. "I changed you to wolf. You needed to be near death, and you were past that point."

"But I'm alive now."

"You are, and when the first full moon comes, you will shift. It will tear your tendons, break your bones, and it will burn, and it will ache, and you'll hate me," Kaylee said with a sigh. "But you will be wolf. And I will meet your wolf."

"I could never hate you, Kaylee. And I want to meet your wolf."

Riaz cleared his throat as he looked between us. "And on that note, be safe." Then Riaz let out a sigh. "More Redwoods are on their way here, Kaylee. To check on you, their new Packmate, and to help us with whatever the fuck happened out on that field."

Memories of Kaylee's scream haunted my waking dreams, and I swallowed hard, knowing that though at this moment I wanted to be near Kaylee, to finish the mating bond and figure out exactly what was happening between us, this wasn't the end.

Someone had tried to kill me. Was he killing others?

Someone was twisting the way that we were looking at rogues now and using it for their own gain.

And if we weren't careful, I wasn't going to be the last casualty in finding out exactly what the hell was going on.

# CHAPTER 16

Kaylee

I WATCHED the door as Riaz walked out, closing it securely behind him. I rolled my shoulders back as my wolf gently pushed to the forefront, wanting control but knowing the human needed the strength here first.

I moved forward, locked the door behind Riaz without even thinking, to keep my mate safe, to keep him locked in. With me.

Then Jason was behind me, his warm breath on the back of my neck, and I pressed my palms to the door, inhaling that deep forest scent that had only increased in its concentration once his wolf had become part of him. I didn't know how he would change once he was turned fully. After his first shift, that scent could change ever so slightly into something more potent, something mine.

"Is it supposed to be like this?" Jason asked, his guttural voice a deep rumble against my skin. My hands dug into the door, my claws sliding out of my fingertips. They tore through the wood of the door, and I let out a shuddering breath. Riaz would have known what he was leaving as he had exited the room. He would know what was happening here.

And I didn't care. I didn't care if the entire Pack stood outside and watched as I claimed my mate as my own.

Was this how it was supposed to be? I wasn't sure, but I could barely focus, could barely breathe.

"What are you feeling?" I asked, my throat so dry it was a rasp.

I may be wet between my legs, but I could barely moisten my lips for speaking.

"Like I want to mount you. Press you hard against the wall, strip your pants down your legs, then fuck you hard until we're both screaming each other's names. I want to mark you. I want to bend you over that table, fuck you hard again. Then lay down as you ride me in all of your glory while I cup your breasts and watch your nipples harden into tight little points. I want them to bounce in my face as I lick them and suck them. I want to spread your ass, lick your hole, then turn you around and fuck your tits, and then come down your throat."

I froze and turned ever so slightly in Jason's hold. And blinked. "All of that? Just tonight? Or stretched out over a few nights?"

Jason blinked, looking so adorably uncertain about what he had just said that I nearly told him that I loved him.

I didn't. I knew I would. Because that's what mating was for. It showed you the person that you would love one day, and you would be with forever. I knew Jason's soul. I knew him inside and out, and I could feel every ounce of who we were in the past and who we could be in the future. But I didn't know him in a way that he could open up to me like that. Not yet. That was the human parts of us, and that would come.

But for now, the fates of mates and the Moon Goddess and whoever else had connected us pulled me to this man. And I knew he was a little embarrassed about what he had just said.

"I didn't think I was going to say all of those words out loud when you asked that question." I watched as the long lines of Jason's throat worked as he swallowed hard. "I mean, I wouldn't do anything that you wouldn't want me to do."

My lips quirked into a smile as I turned fully in his hold and let him pin me to the wall. He caged me with his arms, the thickness of his body. He wasn't slender. He was wide with muscle, even if he wasn't as thick as other wolves. But as I had felt him before, I knew he was thick in all the places that counted.

I held back a groan at that thought, wondering when I had gotten so dirty. I had had sex before. I liked sex. I was damn good at it.

But I didn't like dirty talk.

Except apparently with the cute little geneticist who was about to turn into a wolf, and I wanted him to fuck me hard in the mouth, the pussy, and anywhere else he wanted.

I had become wanton, and I didn't fucking care right then. I might have been a dominant wolf, far more dominant than Jason was at this moment, but it didn't matter. Not with my mate. I was letting him cage me, letting him pin me. And he knew it.

And that just turned us both on.

I leaned forward slightly and cupped his jaw. He was so strong, virile.

"You should know what mating is. What it could be."

He tilted his head, and I held back a smile. That was his wolf. I could sense his wolf, even if I hadn't met him yet. He was wolf now, shifter, but he was still on the precipice of the new part of himself. He would be fighting control for a while, and at this point, when we were still hunting who had killed Spencer and had tried to kill Jason, as well as all of those others, this was a dangerous time for him and everyone else. But I couldn't think about that at that moment. I had to focus on what I was saying.

"I want this. I want you."

"I want you too, Jason. But I need to tell you exactly what mating is. And why we're going about this all backward."

My heart twisted ever so slightly at the thought that I would hurt him with this. That I had already hurt him with this. After all, I had gone about mating this man in a way that might get me shunned with some Packs. Not my own, not the Talons, and clearly not the Starlights. But perhaps older Packs with far more dangerous Alphas. Their control in this new age wasn't as strong as the Alphas that I had grown up with. Or they were along the same lines of Alphas that had nearly wiped out the Packs surrounding me before their current Alphas had taken control.

"What do you mean? I know what mating is."

"Can I please tell you what I feel you need to know before we take this any further?"

He frowned. "You're telling me there's a way to break the bond and go back?"

My body felt as if it had been thrown off a cliff just then, the shock surprising. My wolf growled, and a single fang slid out of my gums. Jason's eyes widened, but he didn't back away. I counted that as a step in the right direction for both of us.

"No, there is no taking it back or changing it. There is no breaking the bond without potentially harming or killing each other in the process. But I want you to know how it should have gone, how we should have come to be." Jason leaned forward again, a small growl reverberating from his throat. He was all wolf just then, and I held back a grin. "Focus, Jason."

"I am focusing." All wolf, and my wolf pawed at me, wanting him.

Soon, I reminded myself. Soon.

"Mates are forever. There's no changing that. You and I had the choice before the attack. We had a choice to walk away, even if it would have hurt. To never see each other again and let the potential fade."

Jason's eyes glowed gold, the dominance in them intriguing.

I couldn't wait to see the man and wolf he would become over the years, as he grew into who he was.

"Never."

"Good, I feel the same way. But we had a choice. And then I took it from you. I took that choice to save your life because it was the only way to keep you in the now. At that moment, even though Riaz was there to help try to save you, it wouldn't have been enough. Changing into a wolf right then wouldn't have been enough. We needed the mating bond to keep you here. To keep you with me." I swallowed hard, the anger and fear culminating in a desperation that gnawed at me.

"I don't regret it. I couldn't regret this. You saved my life, Kaylee."

"And in doing so, I tied you to me and my Pack and my home. I took that choice away from you. And you have to understand that."

"I know. I do. Once we find whoever the hell is attacking our people. Then we can figure out what we need to do from there."

"I don't know if we're going to be able to find out before we need to go to our Alpha. Do you understand that? You are safe and stable here because we are together, but your wolf needs his Alpha. And while Riaz's presence helps slightly as Alpha, he's not your Alpha. You don't have the bonds with this Pack." I grit my teeth. "And I can't be a Starlight. I can't cut my bonds with my family and my Pack members in order to come here and stay here with you. Do you get that?"

He nodded before he frowned and brushed my hair from my face. I nearly leaned into him at the touch, but I needed this moment. I needed him to understand that things were different now, and it wasn't just going to be sex, even though I wanted to strip him down right then and ride him until both of us couldn't breathe anymore.

"I understand. I don't have anyone, Kaylee. I lost my family. It's just me. I'm the friend of the Pack here, but I'm not Pack. I always knew that one day I would grow old and die, and the rest of the Pack would still be here. And I would protect them with whatever I could with my brain, but that was all I had."

"Jason," I began, and he shook his head.

"No, that was it. There is nothing else. I understand that I'm going to have to go up north and meet your family, however big the Jamensons are, because I hear they're a mighty presence in wolves."

He smiled as he said it, and I smiled back. "Perhaps."

"There's no perhaps about it. The War of the Redwoods, and then again with the Talons, is one of legend, one that even I as a human know and have studied and learned. I know parts of who you are, but I want to know the rest. I understand that we are mated, even if it's not complete yet. I get it. I get that sometimes you have to leap into the world of the unknown. I may be a man who always needs answers, but I know when to keep going, to go headfirst, and to find the what-if's later."

I pressed my lips together, trying not to cling to him like a monkey. It was so hard when he was around. "I bit you, my wolf marked you as mine, but once you are fully wolf and can shift, then you need to mark me."

His eyes glowed, and I nearly fell. It was difficult for a wolf pre-shift to glow like that, and it told me of his dominance. I wondered exactly where he would be on the scale once we reached the Redwoods. I wasn't sure, but I was eager to find out.

"And there's sex too, right?" He asked with a tease, and I rolled my eyes.

"You know, I thought you were some just nerdy guy with a nice quiet demeanor who would just follow what I say. Apparently, I was wrong."

He rolled his eyes. "It was the glasses at first, wasn't it? I may be nerdy, but I'm not quiet, and I'm not weak. I never was, Kaylee."

"I never thought you were weak."

"I want you. Tell me more." He leaned forward, deliberately bit down on my lower lip. And I let him.

Because he was mine.

When he moved back, I leaned forward, pressing my breasts to his chest. "Sex will cement the bond between us as humans, and then we're together. Forever. And we have to figure out exactly what that means."

"Good." And then he crushed his mouth to mine. There didn't need to be any more words then. Just mind. And need. And want. He pulled my shirt off quickly, before I could even take my next breath. He crushed his mouth to mine again the instant that he was able and gripped my hips. His hands slid down to cup my ass and pulled me towards him. I jumped, wrapping my legs around him, his thick cock pressed hard against my pussy. "I need you," he growled.

"Good. Because you're about to have me."

We were in a small studio apartment that wasn't ours, but the bed was right there.

He walked me towards it and laid me down on my back. I looked up at him then, cupped my breasts as I grinned. He smiled back, stripped off his shirt, and I sat up, needing him. My claws raked down his jeans, and his eyes widened, but he was so trusting that I wouldn't hurt him that he didn't move. Instead, I tugged away the remnants of his pants and gripped his thick cock in my hands.

"Jesus, I've wanted this."

"Goddess, I've wanted this."

"Good, because you're about to have it." And then he slid his hands through my hair and pressed forward. I opened my mouth, letting the drop of fluid at the tip settle over my tongue before I swallowed the head. He was thick, too thick for me to touch my fingers across, but it didn't matter. He slowly worked his way in and out of my mouth as I leaned forward and took more of him. I used both hands at the base of him, working my head as I went down on him. Jason leaned forward, undid the clasp of my bra, and we both moved to toss it to the side.

And then he was palming my breasts, pinching my nipples, and nearly sending me squirming over the edge. I was still wearing my jeans, and I hadn't thought this through. All I wanted was to feel him, to know him. He was so big in my mouth. It was hard for me to even breathe as I relaxed my throat muscles and slowly took him down deeper.

"Fuck, how can you do that? I'm going to choke you."

I hummed against him and kept going, holding my breath. And when it was too much, I pulled back, the wet sounds nearly sending me over the edge.

I stood up then, still pumping him as I somehow was able to take off my pants, using my claws to rip off my panties. There would be more later. I didn't fucking care; I just needed him.

And then Jason was tossing me on the bed, and I groaned, wanting his dick, but I couldn't. He knelt between my thighs, spread me wide, hard into the bed, so I knew if I were human that he would leave bruises, but I didn't care. Then his mouth was on me, tasting me, and I could barely breathe. My hands tugged at his hair, pressing him harder into me as he lapped me up, spreading my lower folds for him. When he hummed along my clit and speared me with three fingers at once, I nearly came off the bed. But I stopped myself, wanting more. I palmed my breasts, cupping them with eager hands as he kept going, fucking me with his fingers and his mouth. And when I came, my body shook so fiercely I was afraid we were both going to vibrate right off the bed.

I pushed him back on his back and gripped his dick again, needing it in my mouth.

Somehow Jason pulled at my hips, and I was straddling his face as I went down on him, both of us laughing at one another.

"Jesus, I'm going to come," he growled.

I hummed against him, swallowing him as he filled my mouth, the musty taste like ambrosia.

I was losing my damn mind if I thought that, but I didn't care. I just wanted more of him.

We pawed at each other, needing more, and then I was straddling him, gripping the base of his cock and spreading my folds.

"Are you ready?" I asked.

"I've been waiting. Sit down, mate of mine. Let me fuck you."

"I thought that was my line? Let me fuck you, mate of mine."

And I lowered myself in one quick movement.

I let out a sharp bark of breath, both of us freezing as his thickness stretched me to beyond the limits.

"Did you hurt yourself? Are you okay? I'm big, Kaylee. I could have hurt you."

"I'm fine, I'm fine," I said, as he slowly slid his thumb over my clit. The sweet sensation combined with the thickness within me made me come again, and my pussy clamped around his cock.

He groaned and looked up at me. "How can I be so hard again?"

I grinned, leaned down, and kissed him gently. "Because you're a wolf now. It's a perk."

"A damn fine perk."

"I'm going to move," I whispered.

"Good. Ride me. You set the tone. Always."

Tears pricked the back of my eyes, and I swallowed hard. "For now then." And then I moved.

I rode him, both of us clinging to one another before he rolled me on my back and slowly slid in and out of me.

We had started fast, hot, probably a little too hard for a first time between us, but now it was all softness and touching. A gentle sensation that brought us towards climax.

And when my fangs elongated, needing more, the new wolf above me seemed to know what was needed. He tilted his head to the side, and I marked him again over the one I had given him without choice.

Now it was all choice. Now it was who we could be. Once again, the bond snapped into place as he came within me, and I did so around him.

Tears slid down my face as I closed the wound, and he kissed me, and I felt the wetness on his face as well.

I looked up at him then, wondering how this person I barely knew could be mine. The person that I respected, the person I knew who could amount to anything.

He was mine.

"Kaylee," he whispered, and it was as if he was speaking my name for the first time.

"Hi," I whispered, wondering why that was the first thing that came to mind.

He laughed softly, his dick twitching within me as he did. "Hi."

"I should say welcome to the Pack, but maybe hi is a good place to start."

"I think that's a great place to start." He rocked his hips again. "And now let's get to know each other a little bit more. At least until we have to get up, and everything changes."

I knew it was wrong to let us hide from reality for just these moments, but I would be greedy. For just this instant, I would be greedy.

And so we rolled to our sides, both of us arcing into one another as we leisurely made love, both of us finding our rhythm, finding our path.

Reality would come in the morning, but for now, I was getting to know my mate. Even though I knew his soul inside and out, I was falling for the man holding me.

He was wolf. He was mine.

And my wolf was just getting started.

## CHAPTER 17

Jason

THIS IS GOING to be the oddest meet-the-parents anyone has ever had in their lives. At least that's what I was telling myself.

One of Kaylee's fathers and her cousin Parker were about to cross through the wards and come on den land. They were here to not only check on Kaylee, but to take Spencer's body home, as well as help us figure out the next step when it came to those men in black garb who had attacked us and seemed to be the ones attacking our people and leaving those black bite marks everywhere.

Or maybe they were the ones covering up. We didn't

know, but we needed to talk it out, and as Parker was the Voice of the Wolves, and Reed was a strong wolf himself, any cooperation would be helpful.

At least, that's what Riaz had said when he explained to us who was coming. Kaylee hadn't looked surprised, and since they were her family, it made sense.

No, I was the only one really surprised and worried.

After all, they were about to meet Kaylee's mate, a newly made wolf who hadn't even shifted yet and had no idea what the fuck he was doing.

"Come on, we need to meet them," Kaylee said as she tugged on my arm.

I shook my head.

"Maybe you should go to them first alone?"

She frowned, giving me a look. "You want me to meet them without you?"

"I don't want to get in the way."

"How would you be getting in the way? You're my mate, Jason. They're going to love you."

I raised a brow. "I'm not an established wolf, or even a dominant one. I don't know how the hell I'm supposed to protect you or do anything other than make a mess of everything because I don't know what the fuck I'm doing."

Kaylee's eyes glowed gold, and I knew I had said the wrong thing.

"First off, mate of mine, you never need to protect me. I'm dominant enough to protect us both. And yes, I can feel the dominance of your wolf coming along, and one day you may grow to be more dominant than me, and that's perfectly fine. Because you're never going to force that strength on me to try to show me that you're better than me."

I move forward, cupped her face. "Never. I would never do that." I frowned, an odd anger pushing at me. One that was far stronger than I would usually feel.

"Did someone do that to you? I'm sure you already ripped out their throats, but I can come back and do it again once they're healed."

Her lips twitched into a smile before she went on her tiptoes and kissed me softly. "That's very sweet of you, and I like that little aggressive wolf of yours, but don't worry, I'm fine. And you will be fine. My parents will love you. My siblings will love you." She paused. "Well, maybe not Conner."

I gulped. "Your twin?"

"Yes, he's a little growly when it comes to people near me. Mostly because we have that twin bond thing, and I'm going to be the exact same way with whoever comes near him." She shrugged. "We can feel who we are to one another more than most folks. And it hurts to think about somebody hurting our best friend. The other half of us, in the most basic of twin ways."

"Now I'm nervous about meeting Conner."

She grinned. "Don't be. He's going to like you. Not the same way I like you, which is a good thing."

"Yes, that would be a weird thing, considering I'm starting to like you."

I grinned and pulled away, trying to untangle all the emotions pounding through me. It was like everything was on hyperdrive, and I realized it was because of the mating bond, and the fact that I was now a shifter didn't make things any easier for my analytical mind.

"Okay then, let's go meet them, and then we can make a plan to find out exactly who is killing our people and leaving that disease."

I nodded at her. "And frankly, I'm worried about what happens if it spreads."

She froze, staring at me. "It could spread?"

I held up my hands. "I don't know. That's the problem. I'm only partway through my research, and I should have been doing more of it, but then things have been happening, and well, here I am."

"I would say things happen for a reason because that's what fate is, but let's get you back into that lab." She paused. "We're going to have to get you a lab up with the Redwoods."

I swallowed hard. "I guess my life is changing, isn't it?"

She opened her mouth to say something, and I wasn't sure what she could say to make anything feel not so awkward, when a new scent invaded my nose, and Kaylee went to her tiptoes, bounced, and turned to open the door.

"Father," she said, and she wrapped her arms around a man that looked her age, and he hugged her right back.

The guy was tall, wiry, with runner's muscles and sandy hair over his eyes.

"Hey, baby girl." He kissed the top of her head and then moved out of the way so a taller man with broad shoulders and a wide smile could step in, and he hugged her hard. He lifted her off her feet, kissed the top of her head, and Kaylee rolled her eyes at both of them.

I never thought of Kaylee as small. Yes, she was shorter than me, but she had so much power packed within that body of hers, but she never seemed diminutive to me. And yet, seeing her with the two men who had to be her cousin and father, I realized how tiny she was.

And she was all mine.

Damn it.

"Reed, this is my mate, Jason. Jason, this is Reed and

Parker." She looked between us, her voice going slightly high-pitched as she bounced on her toes. "And I've never done this before, so let's not make this awkward. In fact, let's get out of this small room and meet where Riaz is. I thought you guys were going to be out by the wards and not in here."

Reed leaned forward and patted his daughter's hands. "Stop talking so fast. We're not going to hurt your mate.

"Exactly. We aren't Conner," Reed teased, and I looked between the both of them as I stepped closer to Kaylee. Neither Reed nor Parker seemed to care, and my shoulders relaxed marginally. "I'm a little nervous about meeting this Conner."

"Don't be," Reed said. "Conner's growly, and that's because he's a wolf. We're all a bit growly sometimes. My son is just the growliest of my kids."

"But not the growliest of the cousins," Parker said, looking off into the distance.

"I'm never going to get all of your names right, am I?" I asked, as Kaylee slid her hand into mine. My wolf, if that's what I could call it since I wasn't really sure yet, settled down at the touch, and I wanted to find out why. I wanted to look at the science and genetics and peel back the layers as to why that was happening.

But then I remembered that maybe it was magic, and I wasn't supposed to know.

"I can see your mind whirling a million miles a minute. Let's go meet with Riaz and the others, and then we can talk about what we're going to do next." Kaylee squeezed my hand again, pulling me out of my thoughts.

I met Reed's gaze. "If that's okay with you, sir."

Reed's lips twitched into a smile as Parker threw his head back and laughed.

"Oh, I think the family is going to love you, Jason."

"What? You're Kaylee's father. I assumed I'd have to call you sir."

"You're welcome to, but Josh is the growlier one of us. I may be the wolf, but he growls more." Reed winked, and I shook my head, feeling lost and confused but figured I'd have time to figure it out. First, though, I needed to help find whoever the hell was killing our people. Our people. Because it wasn't just the Starlight wolves or their humans or witches. I was wolf too. And they had nearly killed me. And I didn't want to hold back any longer.

We made our way to one of the meeting areas in the den. I hadn't been on Pack lands often, mostly because they always came to me or I met near the den itself with the Pack members that I was friends with.

There had been no real need for me to hang out in

the den, so while I knew certain areas, I had never been in this particular building.

Reed nodded at Riaz, though he didn't lower his gaze. It wasn't a sign of aggression, more that Reed was just that strong. I could feel Riaz's wolf, though, and I knew that Riaz might be the strongest wolf in the room. Reed, Parker, and Kaylee were no slouches either.

It was so odd to be able to feel that, to know that there was a difference, and while I was on the low rung of that ladder for now, my wolf, whatever it was, wanted to get higher.

Things were going to get interesting once I finally shifted.

"We're sorry about Spencer," Riaz began, as Brendan came forward.

"He was yours just as he was ours," Reed said. "But we're here to find out exactly what the hell is going on and how we're going to help fix it. You have the Redwoods and the Talons beside you."

Parker added, "As I'm technically a Talon, I agree with that statement, and both Packs are here to help."

I would have to ask exactly the connections between the two Packs later, but there wasn't time for that right then.

"Jason, tell us what you know," Riaz began, as we all sat down at the table, photos of the dead in front of us and bile rising at my throat. It wasn't that I was squeamish. It was that I was so angry that we couldn't figure this out, and we couldn't stop this, that I was shaking. "Over a year ago now, the Starlight Pack began to find wolves that weren't rogue but were alone out in the forest. They were killed, bitten, and it looked as if they'd got in a fight with another rogue or otherwise killed in a fight. We weren't sure. Either way, though, there were black bite marks around the wounds, as if something gnawed on them, and disease began to take root."

Parker cursed under his breath. "As the Voice of the Wolves, I have contact with every Pack in the world, and I haven't heard about this outside of this area."

I gritted my teeth. "Well, that's a good thing, because we don't want this to be widespread in case it is contagious and becomes a contagion. That means we have someone hunting near the Starlight land."

"And they're taking witches and humans now as well," Riaz added, as a low growl emanated into the room.

It surprised me that it was Kaylee, but she just shrugged. "Sorry, I'm angry."

"Never be sorry for growling in front of wolves," Riaz said with a smile, and I frowned at the other man, wondering if he was flirting with my mate.

Riaz met my gaze for an instant, held up his hands.

"Okay, enough of that while we have two newly mated wolves in the room."

Reed and Parker just shook their heads, their lips twitching, but my wolf wasn't done yet.

"We also need to find out why Spencer was here in the first place," I said, reminding myself that we had a job to do.

"I can help with that," Parker added. "Our wolf came back from the Pittsburgh area, and even though Spencer was supposed to be out there for a work meeting, he never came. But he got a phone call from someone that we don't know to tell him to come out here. It has to be connected to one of those men in the black garb."

"Because if it was one of us, a traitor, they're already dead," Riaz growled.

I frowned, but Kaylee spoke. "I don't think it would be. It doesn't feel right. It feels as if somebody is trying to destabilize us or change the way that we're feeling about rogues. There's already an increased rogue presence around the world, and that could be due to the shift in power from the Supreme Alphas coming and the Moon Goddess and the wars that we've had." She let out a breath. "But this seems like an additional thing. As if something that is trying to take advantage of the already tumultuous presence we have with the additional rogues."

"I agree," Riaz said. And then he looked at me. "We need to find out if these bite marks are contagious, if it can spread if the wolf or human or witch doesn't die from the bite itself. And we need to find out exactly who's doing this."

"They have to be close. After all, they were close enough to get me."

"And that means they're watching you. They knew you getting close to something," Kaylee whispered. She squeezed my hand.

"So we'll have to fight back, get close enough so that they think they have the upper hand, and then we take them down," Reed growled.

I met their gazes and nodded. "Then we hunt, we make a plan, and we use science and whatever else we can to take them down."

"You sound like a wolf," Kaylee said softly. "And I like it."

I met her gaze, then the others, and the bond flared between Kaylee and me.

We would find out who had done this to Spencer and who was going to try to do this to the others.

I couldn't let any of my Pack die; I couldn't let them get hurt.

We needed to find out who was doing this and stop them. I had to be the last casualty in this war because something else was coming, we all knew it, but first we needed to find out who was taking out our wolves and why.

# CHAPTER 18

Jason

THE FULL MOON hit the next day. There would be a hunt with the Starlights for some, with Reed and Parker joining them. I would be with Kaylee, near the edge of the run in case we needed help, but honestly, I didn't want everyone to see me shift for the first time. I would need the strength of an Alpha, and Riaz would be close by, but here I was, my wolf prowling inside, pushing at me, and the tension so thick I could barely breathe.

"We've been searching along this grid and have come up with nothing, but there has to be someone. We have to find where these people are coming from and what these bites are from." Riaz pinched the bridge of his nose as he spoke and paced. His wolf had to be riding him as well on night of the full moon right before we shifted.

It wasn't that shifters needed the full moon to shift. They could do it at any time. Sometimes, depending on their strength, they could only do it once a day and would remain in either wolf or human form, depending on what they had shifted into. However, the dominant wolves around me could shift a few times a day as long as they kept their food intake up.

For the first shift, for my first shift, I needed the strength of the Moon Goddess. That meant I would need that strength from the brightest night of connection to her—the night of the full moon.

I could feel it beckoning me, waiting for me to go outside and do whatever I needed to do.

I wasn't scared. I would be with Kaylee and the others around me. This was natural for them, and soon it would be natural for me. First, however, I needed to learn to breathe again.

"While we're on the hunt, we'll be looking at this next grid," Brendan added, as Parker and Reed looked down at the man, nodding.

"It's a good plan." Parker frowned. "They're hiding

somewhere, and it has to be in plain sight. You guys aren't slouches when it comes to the hunt."

Riaz snorted. "Glad you think so, Voice of the Wolves."

Reed just rolled his eyes. "I swear Parker was like this when he was a little boy and came to live with us, too."

I frowned at that, wondering at the history, but nobody seemed surprised about it. I had so many questions about these wolves and their histories, but considering some were centuries old, I would never keep up with all the lives they had lived.

And now it seemed, as long as I didn't die in my first shift or in a war, I would live centuries as well.

I swallowed hard.

"What's wrong?" Kaylee asked, as everyone looked at me.

I cringed. "Sorry. I was thinking about how my life is completely different. What I'm about to do and I have the possibility of living for centuries instead of only a few short decades. That's a lot of time to study on my work."

Kaylee rolled her eyes. "Of course, that's what you would think."

"I don't know. An age-old geneticist could come up with brilliant breakthroughs." Reed smiled. "Or in a century, you could change your mind to become an artist like me. Or you could be anything that you want to be. We'll have to talk soon about setting up your lab or whatever you need up north, but for now, we should probably get outside. So you can find your wolf, and then we can find the bastards that are hurting our own."

He growled as he said it, his eyes glowing gold. I had never heard Reed growl like that, not in the few short days I had known him. Kaylee just grinned as her father did so, and Parker's eyes glowed, and then the Starlights did as well.

My wolf reared up, pushing at me, and I let out a sharp breath. "Okay then. Um. Is it supposed to hurt like this?"

Pain radiated at my side, and Kaylee cringed. "It's going to hurt worse. I'm sorry. Shifting is beautiful, but it's not easy. It's painful."

"And the first shift is always going to be the hardest because of the unknown," Riaz said as he came forward. "But we'll be here with you."

"We'll be there in the trees," Reed corrected, as Parker nodded.

"Kaylee will be the only one in your sight, so you're not self-conscious," Brendan added.

"However, eventually, you are going to get used to shifting in front of others. The social norms of humans aren't the same with us wolves," she paused. "I'm not sure about the cats."

I let out a breath, telling myself that this is just one step. The first step for the rest of my life. Then why did it feel as if I were being thrown off a cliff rather than just taking a step?

I found myself outside, stripped down to the skin in front of Kaylee. It felt odd to be naked under the moonlight, but then I looked down at my very naked mate and swallowed hard. "Oh. I think I could like this part."

Kaylee rolled her eyes. "Most shifters don't notice nudity in this case. But we're mates, so we're allowed to. Just know that while my father and cousins aren't watching us, they will be able to hear us during the shift. So be careful."

I blinked. "Well, that just put a downer on anything."

My cock still twitched looking at her, and Kaylee's eyes glowed gold as she trailed her gaze down my body.

"After."

"After we shift back?"

Kaylee cringed. "Yes. After we shift back. Only sex as humans, though I thought you already knew that."

"I did. It was just nice to have it confirmed."

Kaylee let out a snort. Then I reached out to try to

grab her hand. A spasm of pain rocketed me, and I let on a sharp breath. "Shit."

"Down on your hands and knees, now. This is what I want you to do." She put her hands on my shoulders and looked right into my eyes as she knelt before me. I had to do my best not to stare at her breasts or any other part of her. However, the pain was so intense inside me it was becoming easier and easier with each passing moment. "What I want you to do is to breathe through this. To pull on that slight tug you feel between yourself and your wolf. It's going to be different than the cord that connects you as a human. And it will be different from the that connects us as mates. But it's something there, a jagged edge, something rugged. Something that is just yours. Whatever's pushing at you, grab for it, and hold on."

I met her gaze, the green of them soothing as well as intoxicating. And then, as I did as she said, imagining that thread that connected me with my wolf, it snapped its jaws down on the thread, and I let out a pained howl.

"There you go. It's waiting. There you go, breathe. Now you can do this. Push again, and your wolf will know what to do. Just lean into the change. It will guide you, and I will be here for you throughout it all. I promise." Then she leaned down, pressed her lips to mine, and I closed my eyes, pulling at the bond between my wolf and me.

Everything shifted at that point. A bright light behind my eyes nearly blinded me. Bones broke, tendons tore, my muscles raged, and I let out a scream that turned into a pure howl.

It felt like nothing I'd ever been through before, nothing I had ever known.

My wolf nudged at me, looking at my face as if trying to soothe me through the hurt. As I looked down, everything was so much brighter, different.

I blinked, looked down at my white paws, and then up into the face of my mate.

Tears stained her cheeks, and she leaned forward, kissed my muzzle, because now I had a muzzle, and beamed. "You are all white. Gorgeous. I'm glad that you're moving up north and not staying down here in Texas, because you're going to blend in much more up there. You are gorgeous. Pure white, with bright blue eyes and a tiny black dot right on your tail. I'll take photos one day for you, but first I need to shift. And then we run."

I took a step toward her, slightly wobbly, and she kissed my cheek. "Let your wolf guide you. You'll still be there. Your wolf won't be in control. I can feel the strength with you, the dominance. You have this. You are a strong wolf, high in the hierarchy. And as soon as you meet my Uncle Kade, our Alpha, you'll know where you fit. I can't wait to see you soar. Thrive." Then she kissed me again before she shifted. She was a dark black wolf with slightly red-brown edges along her fur. Her eyes were that bright green of hers, and she was gorgeous. She was slightly smaller than me even though she was a tiny ball of muscle. She bounced around me, wanting to play, and then a large red wolf came through the forest, followed by a few more wolves. It was the Pack, and we were running.

Riaz, as the largest of the bunch, his power radiating, came forward, and I lowered my gaze instinctively. Kaylee did the same. We were guests on Pack land, and while we would never submit to this Alpha, we would not encroach on his territory.

Then Riaz threw his head back in a howl, and we joined him. My wolf radiated glee, as if this is where I had been supposed to be my entire life. I had been born human, but I was meant to be a wolf.

And then we ran.

The dirt touched against the pads of my paws, and then I moved, following Kaylee as I stumbled once, and then again, and then finally I did what my mate told me, and I let the wolf go.

We jumped over a fallen log through the wild oaks

that dotted the landscape. It wasn't the greenery of the Pacific Northwest, but we were in the hill country of Texas. There were trees and green, but the dirt was warm, even in the setting sun and rising moon.

We ran, my wolf in glee as my bond between Kaylee flared, and I could feel her wolf tugging at it, wanting to meet her mate as well. She circled me as we veered off from the others, yipping madly as she looked at my face and bowed her head. She stuck her tail up in the air and danced a bit, and I knew she wanted to play. So I jumped at her, nipping her playfully as she growled a bit, and began to chase me. I turned, chasing her back, enjoying the feel of wind in my fur as we let the moon dance around us.

Somehow I was wolf. Somehow I was Pack.

And this was my mate.

When Kaylee moved forward and nipped at me again, I paused, wondering what she was doing. And then she stood still for a second before she began to shift back, her human body sweat-slick, naked, and sexy as hell.

"Pull the bond, Jason. You have the power, the strength to shift back. You won't need to stay wolf all night."

And I wanted to be with my mate. I needed to be. So I did as she said, the pain a sweet agony as it had been before. And then I was naked, sweaty, and hard as fuck.

Kaley grinned at me, but before she could pin me, I pushed her back into the soil, her legs spread beneath me, and I grinned. "Ready to play some more?"

She nipped at my lip.

"I thought you'd never ask."

And then I kissed her, plunging deep inside her wet heat.

# CHAPTER 19

Kaylee

I SPREAD MY LEGS MORE, Jason sliding deeper into me. I groaned, arching up into my mate as he licked along my neck and bit down gently. He wasn't using his fangs. He wouldn't be able to yet, but soon. Maybe later tonight, or another time. We had already mated, already marked each other, and our bond tugged on us true. We were mates. I wanted him to mark me. I wanted to wear my hair on the top of my head and show the mark of being his. Never in my wildest dream would I imagine that's what I would want with another person, that I would want someone touching me and marking me and claiming me as theirs. That I would want others to know that I had given in, that I had submitted. But here I was, wanting it. Wanting my mate.

He bit down again, and I knew I would bruise slightly, and I craved it. Then he went to my breasts, sucking and laughing at me, and I groaned, my wolf at the forefront, my eyes glowing gold, and I grinned.

This was what I had been missing. I had been fighting my entire life to find some form of semblance of who I was or who I could be. I had tried to make sure that I had a purpose, that I wasn't just the Triad's daughter. That I wasn't just a strong female in a Pack of strong wolves.

I had tried to find out who I was, and in essence I had, but there had always been something missing. And it wasn't a man. It wasn't me wanting to fall in love so all of my answers could be with me.

No, it was the idea of finding a future that I could follow while being myself.

Jason wasn't just the one in control; I was as well.

He would be a partner and help me, and he was everything.

And he bit me on my nipple.

I growled, my wolf looking through my eyes as I glared at him.

"Hey."

"Pay attention to me. I'm balls deep inside of you, and you're growling. And it's not the fun type of growl. I've been learning what the fun type of growl is."

"I'm sorry, I'll pay more attention. I promise." I squeezed my inner muscles, and he groaned before he lapped up my nipple. We both sighed, our bodies shaking as they came together.

He was just so sweet. And far more dominant than I was expecting. I liked it. He slid deep into me again, both of us arching into one another as the heat of the hunt slid over us, the moon beckoning us. We didn't need a full moon to run as a Pack, and most of the time we didn't run on the full moon. Not unless there was a ceremony, or we needed the connection. This run wasn't just for our mating. It wasn't just because this was Jason's first shift. This was because Pack needed the togetherness and attachments after everything that had happened.

And here I was, with my mate, and I wanted it to be perfect. I wanted everything to just *be*.

We turned, and he flipped me over, so I was on top, and I looked down on him, pushing my hair back from my face.

"Really?"

"If you're going to fade off into the distance, I'm not doing it right. Fuck me, woman."

I threw my head back and laughed before I rolled my hips.

Jason slid his hands up to my hips and squeezed, keeping me steady, and I looked down at him, and then he looked at his hips, pummeling into me as he was the one in control even if I was on top.

I dug my claws into his shoulders, just slightly, and he groaned. I couldn't help but love the fact that he seemed to be enjoying himself just like I was. "You're a goddess," he growled, before he flipped me over again, and I found myself on all fours.

He gripped my hips, this time his claws slightly peeking out of his fingertips. The sensation sent me over the edge, just slightly, and I came, clamping down at his cock as he continued to hammer into me.

"Jason," I growled.

"That's it. Keep going. We're not even close to being done yet."

"That is the endurance of a wolf, just you wait, mate of mine. Your claws are showing."

Jason froze for a second, his claws sliding back into his fingertips. Neither one of us were ready for that or what would happen if he lost control, but he was gaining control so quickly.

He was a thinker, he wasn't soft, and he would be a fighter. And I was falling for him. Just like that, I was falling for him. I couldn't wait to fall deeper, to find out exactly who he was and who we could be together.

I groaned up into him, pushing back, needing more. And when he flicked his fingers over my clit, I came again, and he followed me, this time with me leaning back up into him, so my back was to his front, one hand over my pussy, the other hand over my breasts.

"You're so fucking beautiful," he growled into my ear.

I let out of shaky breath. "I can't believe I just had sex outside after a hunt with a Pack that's not our own, and it's with my mate."

He chuckled, letting out a breath that tickled my neck. "You think you're shocked. I have no idea how the hell I got here."

We made love again, both of us going slow, the moon egging us on. Our wolves needed this, just as much as the humans, but maybe this time was for the wolves.

And when we finished, we cleaned up in the nearby creek and changed into clothes that smelled distinctly of Riaz.

Jason growled and put the sweats up to his nostrils. "Is that? I know that scent."

I beamed, loving the way that he was leaning into these new talents and senses of his.

"Yes, that is Riaz."

He frowned as he handed them over. "Am I supposed to like you smelling just like another man?"

I sighed. "I don't smell like him. It's just a contact layer from him setting it down. They're our clothes. I'm not going to smell like him in a minute once it dissipates. And you're not going to smell like him either. I'm just as territorial. Just making sure you understand that."

His eyes glowed gold. Damn it. His wolf was so freaking controlled even after such a short time. I couldn't help but smile at them both. "I see. Good to know. And now that I can focus a little bit more, the scent of Riaz has dissipated." He paused. "So he was around for all of that?"

I rolled my eyes. "No, he was doing his own thing. I didn't scent anyone around us, so I have a feeling that they gave us some space. At least my father and my cousin weren't the ones that handed off the clothes, because what would be a whole other set of questions."

Jason winced, and I went up to my tiptoes to kiss him. I slid my feet into my shoes, and I watched as Jason put his knife in his boot.

He was good with a knife, I remember that, but he was going to have to learn how to fight like a wolf. Not tonight, though, and maybe not tomorrow. When we got to the Redwood Pack. When it was going to be completely changing his life, and I was going to have to figure out how that was going to happen.

"Let's get back to the others?" Jason asked as he leaned forward, cupping my cheek. "Are you going to tell me what's got that look in your eyes?"

I bit my lip. "I'm taking you from everything. I know you said you have no family here and you want to go back with me to where I'm from, but everything is changing in a blink, Jason. I wasn't expecting you. You weren't expecting me. And yet I'm forcing you to make huge decisions."

"I'm pretty sure the Moon Goddess is the one that made the original decision, but we finished that choice. You and me."

Guilt crept up my throat, and Jason shook his head.

"I see that look again. You saved my life, and you saved us. I get that. Now stop. Stop wondering what could have been because that's not going to be it. This is you and me. Yes, I'm moving, and I'm mated, and it makes no sense, but we'll have a lifetime, lifetimes for that matter, to figure out what it is." He ran his hands through his hair, and I did my best to stop watching the way that his muscles bunched and moved. "I have no idea what the fuck I'm going to do, Kaylee. But I know I'm going to do that by your side. I'm going to need you to protect me from all your siblings. And your dad and your father and your mom. And all of your cousins. And your uncles And every other member of the Packs up there. It's a little daunting. I have no one, Kaylee. But you have so much."

I wiped tears from my face, unaware I was even crying until just then. "You'll have them too. Once we figure out exactly what we're going to do. I came here to find a rogue, to find Spencer." I swallowed hard, that familiar sorrow etching its way over my soul. "I found him, but not in the way that I wanted. And now we're going to find answers. Soon. I can feel it. And then we'll go home. You and me. And we'll find a way to make this work. In this new world of ours."

Jason leaned forward, pressed his lips to mine. "In this new life of ours. I want to continue my work. I can feel it within me, this wolf pushing at me and telling me that I have this power and this strength, but I don't want to fuck it up. So I'm going to need you to make sure that doesn't happen."

"I think you're going to get along with my twin."

He blinked. "What do you mean by that?"

"Connor says that often. About his relationship with his wolf. I think you two will have a lot to talk about." I patted his cheek. "And I promise you my twin will not maim you. He'll growl, but he growls at everyone. It's a sign of love."

Jason winced. "Good thing you're warning me. Now I guess we should get back?"

I started to say something before Jason scrunched his nose. "What's that smell?"

I blinked, my claws sliding out of my fingertips once more. "Get your knife, Jason."

The acrid scent of death came for us, and I whirled, ducking out of the way of a claw.

Was it a claw? It looked like a hand, with four fingers and a long thumb. There were talons on the ends of them, but the rest of it looked like a man, but with a hunchback, slanted eyes, and hair on its shoulders, neck, and part of its scalp. Its legs bulged, and one knee was backward, the other forward.

Honestly, I wasn't sure how it was even moving.

It growled at me, and I cursed under my breath before I slashed my claws at it.

"I think it's alone. Go get the others."

"I'm not leaving you," Jason growled, getting his knife out of his boots. He swung it forward, slicing at the rogue in front of me, but could I call it a rogue?

It looked like nothing I had seen before. It wasn't man. It wasn't wolf. It was something else.

And from the black tar on its teeth, it had to be part of what was killing around us.

The deformed wolf growled at us, snapped its jaws before it howled into the air and jumped.

I didn't know what its bite or its claws would do to us, so I rammed my shoulder into its side, pushing it out of the way so it wouldn't get at Jason or me. I tried to get at its flank, slicing my claws along its belly, but it kept moving. Its hide far tougher than a normal wolf's.

Jason tossed his knife, and it slammed into the wolf's back. The wolf reared back in howling anger, but it kept going.

I cursed under my breath, shaking my head.

"What was that?" I asked.

"I don't know. But I'm really glad it didn't fucking bite you."

I looked at Jason, and as Riaz and the others ran out of the forest, some in wolf form, some naked in human form, I knew we were in trouble.

Because that wasn't a rogue.

And something in the back of my mind clicked.

"The serum," I said, and looked over at my father.

Reed, fully clothed, shook his head. "We need to talk to Kade."

The Alpha of the Redwood Pack would know, and Riaz should know as well.

"What serum?" Jason asked, before his eyes widened. "*That* serum."

"Yes. That serum."

The serum that the humans had made a few years ago to try to make a werewolf of their own.

But werewolves weren't science; they weren't shifters who could be turned with chemicals.

There might be enzymes involved, an actual physical transition.

The serum tried to use science when it was magic that caused the shifter to become who they were.

My cousin's mate was one of those who had survived. I had thought he was the only one who had survived, and only because the serum hadn't truly worked, it had been the Talon Pack who had saved him.

And when we explained this to Jason, he scowled and pulled out his phone. "I have to look at my notes, but this isn't good."

I looked at my family, at the Starlight Pack, and shook my head.

"No, it isn't good."

Because if that thing was from the serum, it had to be a new amalgamation of chemicals. A new try. And I had a feeling if we weren't careful, if we didn't catch whoever was doing this, it would only be the beginning.

The beginning that screamed of death.

# CHAPTER 20

Jason

MY WOLF PACED beneath my skin, not wanting out but wanting answers. It was odd to have this new life, this new strength within me that I didn't understand. I could pick up a suitcase with just my pinky that once I'd have to grunt over. My strength was increasing day by day, my senses nearly overwhelming. And yet, my wolf was oddly calm. Not aggressive, not pushing at others. Rather, it could soothe me with all of these extra senses and awareness around me.

I wasn't sure if this was how mating and turning into

a wolf was supposed to go, but here I was, and this was my life.

It was odd, and yet it was mine.

I needed to figure out what I was supposed to do next.

What I wanted to do next, though, had nothing to do with my wolf, nothing to do with my mate, other than protecting them both.

"You're scowling. Do you want to talk about it?" Reed asked as he leaned against the doorway. I stood in my lab, frowning over the results from underneath Kaylee's nails.

"Talk about what?" I asked, scowling.

"Your first hunt. You didn't get a chance to decompress most of what you went through."

I looked up at Kaylee's father and shook my head. "There's not much to say. I changed into a wolf, I shifted, and here I am." There was more, but I wasn't sure when I'd be ready to find my answers. I was an analytical man, or at least I had been. Reconciling those two parts of myself wouldn't be easy, but I'd need time to do so, and I wasn't ready yet. Even with the gentle yet steel-spined wolf at my side.

Reed smiled softly as if reading my thoughts. "Here you are. I have to say, compared to how some of my family members turned into wolves, sometimes not of their own choosing, you're handling this far better than I would have."

"You were born a wolf, weren't you?"

"I was. Over two centuries ago."

My eyes widened. "Really." I wanted to know more about these wolves, about all magics I couldn't understand, but I wasn't sure where I belonged.

"Why do I feel like you want to look at me under a microscope?" Reed asked dryly.

I shrugged, looking at my next slide. "It'd be interesting. Though I think Riaz is older than you. And I've already looked at him underneath a microscope."

Reed blinked, smiled again. "He let you?"

"I wanted a baseline for what I was searching for. That deformed human or wolf or whatever it is. I wanted to know so I could help find it. I didn't know it was going to be like this."

"I don't think any of us did. I've never seen anything like that in my long years."

I looked up at the other man. "Truly?"

"Truly, and I've seen a lot of things. I've seen demons and witches. I've seen the end of our earth, a fiery blaze that could scorch the ruins of who we are. I've seen wars and battles. I've seen loss and births." Reed smiled, and it lit up his entire face. "Did Kaylee tell you that I fell on my ass when the babies were born?" he asked, and I shook my head.

"No. We haven't had a chance to talk about much of her life."

Reed gave me a look, and I didn't lower my gaze, but telling the man in front of me that I'd mostly been spending my time either naked with Kaylee or trying to find the deformed shifter, might not be the best thing.

"Josh and I fell on our asses when Conner and Kaylee were born. My wife loves to make fun of us for it."

The thought made me grin, my shoulders easing. "And then you proceeded to have a few more kids. Did you fall for them?"

"No, probably because it was the whole twin thing."

"Kaylee has all this energy and power. I can't even imagine with two of them."

"Don't even get me started. Conner is this steadfast growl of a man. He's honorable, almost to a fault some-times. Kaylee is a quiet power, a determination that surprises me with each moment of every day. All of my children surprise me in the best ways." Reed let out a breath.

"When you come up north, you'll have to meet with the Alphas, and not just the Redwood Alpha, my brother Kade."

I turned to him and frowned. "Because you think I have to, need to, or something else?" I asked, confused why Reed would bring that up.

"Because it would be interesting to see how you deal with all of them. You're a very calm wolf, Jason. You're like my brother, Maddox, when he was the Omega. Not that you are an Omega, the one that can help soothe emotions or control them or deal with the excess emotions that can threaten a Pack. But you do have a soothing part of your soul. I wonder who you will be when the time comes."

"I don't know about that," I said, frowning. "There's just the two Alphas, though, right? The Redwood Pack and the Talon Pack?"

"We're also allies with the new Centrals and the Aspens."

"Weren't the Centrals part of the war with you?" I asked, confused, and hoping I wasn't stepping on toes.

Something went over Reed's gaze, and he nodded. "Yes, and then they were decimated. They're back, though, learning their ways. Just like the Aspens are learning how to be who they are with their new structure. Things are changing, with the rogues, a darkness we can sense, but our packs are working together. Parker's down here not only to find vengeance for Spencer but to work with Riaz and the Starlight Pack. We have connections with the Thanes Pack over in England. We are doing our best to create allies where we can because something is coming."

"And you don't think it's this rogue that isn't a rogue."

Reed shook his head. "Not anymore. And that worries me."

"Because if it's not this, that means there's something else out there."

"Something is creating these rogues or pushing them or something. And we must figure it out."

"I've got it, Father," Kaylee said as she rushed in, her phone in her hand. Riaz, Brendan, and more of the Starlights followed. "We figured out who called Spencer. It's a human, one who's been on our radar for a while but went underground."

I frowned, my wolf on edge as soon as Kaylee walked into the room.

"Who?"

"Kyle. Lieutenant Kyle Moore."

Reed's eyes glow gold, and I frowned as others filled my small little lab.

"Who's that?"

"Kyle is one of the men who we couldn't find after the general was killed."

"As in, the general who helped make the serum trying to make their own shifters?"

Kaylee's hand slid into mine. "One and the same. Kyle lured Spencer down here for some reason."

"To get you down here?" Riaz asked, frowning. "Or at least, one of the Redwoods. The Talons? You're all practically one big Pack up there. He tried to lure you guys down here for a reason."

"Revenge?" I asked, frowning.

"Maybe, or maybe he's lost his god damn mind," Parker growled. "Either way, we have his name, we have where he is, and we're going to find him."

"I have some good news," I put in, clearing my throat as the weight of an Alpha and dominant wolves leveled me.

I didn't bow down, though I did lower my gaze, just in case. "Whatever it is, it isn't contagious. It took me a while to finish this test, but these bites? It's trying to make its own wolf as the original wolves did back in that story Kaylee told me. But it's not working. They can't create their own wolves. They can just kill. Not that there's anything *just* about killing."

"So that black tar crap isn't contagious?" Brendan asked, frowning as he moved forward.

"Really."

Kaylee frowned. "That's good to hear, but he's still killing people out there."

Riaz shook his head. "Trying to form an army or revenge or something."

"And we're going to have to stop it," Riaz growled.

"Damn straight we are," Riaz growled.

Dean ran into the room just then, seemingly surprised so many people were in my lab.

"What is it?" Riaz asked.

"Seven men, all dressed in black, tranq guns at the ready. They're at the edge of the wards. And my senses are tingling. Something's out there."

Kaylee cursed. "The mutant. It's here, and we're going to have to take it down."

"All of us, together," Riaz said, his voice a growl.

I picked up my knife, spun it in my hands. "I can fight like this. I think I'm going to need training how to fight the other way."

Reed's eyes glowed gold. "We've got you. Up in the Redwoods."

Riaz narrowed his eyes. "Since you are a Redwood, that would make sense. We can talk about it later."

Reed and Riaz met gazes before they both broke the connection, and we made our way outside.

Kaylee was at my side, and I frowned. "What is it?" I asked.

"Nothing but dominance games, but be careful. Do you understand me?"

"Of course, I'm going to be careful. You will do the same." It was an order, and she didn't seem to mind.

"No, stay at my side. You can fight with a knife, sure, but I'm not going to let you get hurt."

"And I'm not going to let you either." I tugged her arm, then crushed my mouth to hers. She growled against me but didn't push me away.

"So not the time," she growled.

"I know. But we're going to figure this out. Together."

And at the first broken howl, the first growl that sliced the air, I knew that our time was here.

We wouldn't have to go out and find the mutant wolf.

He had found us.

# CHAPTER 21

Jason

I COULD SENSE the wrongness right outside the wards. Riaz and his wolves were ready for what was coming, we weren't alone, and we had to take it down.

"Stay at my side," Kaylee ordered, and since she knew what she was doing, and I was only somewhat trained, I would listen to her.

"I would rather have you safe behind the wards, but I know that Riaz wants to make sure that we get samples and firmly knock down whatever this is. So you have to be here."

I rolled my shoulders back, blade in hand. "Sounds like a plan to me."

Then the mutant wolf crawled forward, black drool sliding down its fangs as it came towards us.

"Dear goddess," Parker mumbled from my side as he shook his head. "That's monstrous."

"Just a little bit," Riaz growled.

"Are you getting pictures?" Parker asked, as Reed began to snap photos. "Yes, but we can't let the rest of the world know about this."

"No, we take care of it. Together."

When the rogue mutant slid his hand across the wards, I could hear the searing of flesh, but it didn't back down. It wouldn't.

It didn't understand.

There were others with him, not mutants, but those men with the tranq guns, and we needed to stop whatever was happening before it got worse. Before they killed any more people than they already had.

I didn't know what was going to happen next, or the plan, other than for me to stay by Kaylee's side, but then one of the soldiers in black came forward, his hand around the throat of a teenager.

Everyone froze, and Riaz let out a growl so low it made my own wolf cower. I nearly went to my knees, and Kaylee did the same.

I had never heard the power of an Alpha with that voice before, and I never wanted to hear it again.

"Elijah?" Riaz asked.

"I'm sorry," Elijah whispered, his voice low.

"Elijah doesn't live in the wards. He lives with his human grandparents an hour away."

"His parents?" Kaylee asked, her voice barely above a whisper.

"They were two of the wolves taken down by this monster," I whispered.

Pain filled her eyes, and I swallowed hard. Elijah was a wolf but wasn't fully into his strength yet. And somehow, this man had gotten him. The team was trying to lure Riaz and the others out. And from the way that Riaz was ready to take anyone down just then, it might've worked.

"Come out here, Alpha, let's play. Then you can have your little wolf Pack."

"Kyle," Kaylee snapped.

"We have to make sure that there's no more serum. That we destroy it all. Before we kill him," I reminded everybody.

The Beta, Brendan's gaze snapped towards me, but the other wolf just nodded tightly. "We'll get the answers, and then we'll get that mother fucker's throat."

Riaz took one step outside of the wards, the strength

of the Alpha so dominating I had to suck in a breath. "Let my wolf go."

"Fight my wolf first, and then we have a deal."

Things happened quickly after Elijah screamed, went to the ground, and everybody moved.

It was as if it had been a coordinated effort even though I knew it wasn't, just instinct. My own wolf pushed at me, and we made our way through the wolves. I slammed my blade into the nearest soldier as he came for me, his gun raised towards Kaylee.

Kaylee growled, took the gun in hand, and bent it in half, her strength sexy as hell. The man was still screaming, so she reached out and snapped his neck before we went to the other one.

The rogue was in front of us though, the mutant that wasn't wolf, wasn't rogue, wasn't human. He was something other.

He scented like something I couldn't tell, but he was circling Kaylee and me while the others fought Kyle and the others at his side.

"Kill it, but don't let it bite you," Kaylee growled, and then we were off.

The mutant clawed at Kaylee, but she shoved out of the way, raking her claws down its side.

Parker was there by her side then, the two of them fighting as if they'd been doing this their whole lives.

I pulled my blade out of the dead soldier and aimed at the rogue's spine. If I could get him to stop moving, then maybe we could stop this wolf completely.

I aimed true, the blade sliding into the mutant's back, and when it howled, it went to his knees, and the other wolves went to work.

The fight was quick, bloody, and the soldiers were far outnumbered. I didn't know what they thought they would get out of this.

This wasn't a battle. It wasn't a war. This was suicide.

And the soldiers seemed to have known it going in.

I found myself standing over a dead mutant, its eyes glazed over, and I had to wonder who it had been. What it had been before it had either volunteered or been forced to take a serum that clearly didn't work.

I looked over at Riaz, who had his claws around Kyle's neck.

"Are there any others?" Riaz asked his voice low, demanding.

"Like I would tell you," Kyle growled out. His legs were broken, his arms pinned back. He wasn't getting out of this alive. Not only had he killed people, but he had also threatened a pup. That alone would be a death sentence in the world of wolves, but he had killed witches and humans and wolves. He deserved what was going to happen next. And for someone who had grown up human, I didn't feel a lick of pity.

I couldn't.

"Why?" Kaylee asked, her voice a growl beside the other man.

Kyle just grinned, and I stood over him, recognizing the man's face. "I know you. You came into the lab once."

Riaz gave me a sharp look, but then focused back on Kyle.

"I thought maybe you could help. Help us to find the serum that the general had used. But you were worthless. A friend of the Pack. I wanted the Redwoods to pay. I wanted them to know what they had done, just like the Talons. So I lured Spencer out here. And he's dead. And I'm glad for it. All of you deserve to die. Deserve to end where you are because you are abominations. Jene sacrificed himself for us, tried to become the wolf that he is, but he was as worthless as all of you."

"Is there any more serum?" I asked, tilting my head as I studied his face.

"Of course there is."

I tasted the lie, wondering how I could know it, and Riaz shook his head.

"He's lying."

"I know."

Kaylee growled low. "You killed Spencer. You killed so many others. But we found your lab. We've killed your men, and you're done now. You're never going to hurt another person again."

"You aren't people, whore."

My wolf raged, and I moved forward, bloody blade in hand. But Riaz held up a hand.

"No, I've got this." And with a twitch of his hand, a snap echoing in the air, Kyle was no more.

Those who had attacked our people, had butchered them, leaving black and bloody claw marks and bite marks all over them, were gone.

I let out a breath and met Kaylee's gaze, hoping this was truly the end.

By the time we cleaned everything up, more of Riaz's wolves had checked out the compound where the soldiers had stayed.

They had indeed used up the last of their serum, and perhaps they had wanted me to help them. But I was a geneticist. There was only so much I could do. Not that I would've ever turned against the Packs.

They had been my family long before I turned wolf, and I was only just now realizing that.

I stood in a clearing with Riaz, Kaylee with her

father a few yards beside us, going over the flight plans for when we can leave.

"They were here because they thought they could hide from us. Because our Pack isn't as connected to the other Packs as the Pacific Northwest is, or even those on the East Coast. That's going to have to change." Riaz frowned.

"You're already changing it. Parker's here."

Riaz nodded. "You're right. It is."

"Something I don't get through. If these weren't the rogues that we know keep popping up, then what else are we missing? What aren't we getting?"

Riaz met my gaze and shook his head. "I don't know. But something's out there, and it's not these soldiers. Something else had magic to keep us away before, when you were attacked. Something held enough magic to allow the mutant to get closer to the wards than he should have. The soldiers weren't working alone. Or something was helping them. And I want to know what it was."

I knew there was a worry spreading through the Packs, and not just the one in front of me. Rogues were a danger to everyone around them, and they were increasing in occurrence with each passing year.

Something was changing them, something pulling

them towards their more animalistic and uncontrolled sides.

I didn't know what it was, but we would have to find out.

"I'm sure you'll keep looking," Riaz began. "Up with the Redwoods."

I winced. "Is that okay? That I'm Redwood and not Starlight?"

Riaz reached out and squeezed my shoulder, his wolf so strong I wanted to bow down just then. It was an odd feeling, and I wasn't sure I liked it.

"Go. They will be your family. Maybe you'll finally let yourself be with them, rather than on the outskirts that you were with us."

I winced. "It was never anything about any of you."

"I know." Riaz looked over my shoulder at Kaylee. "You needed that push. And Kaylee's it. But just know, when you go, you might be theirs, but your ours now, too. Just like Spencer was."

He swallowed hard, and I knew he had said it loudly for Kaylee and Reed's benefit.

I met the Alpha of the Starlight Pack's gaze and knew this wouldn't be the last I'd see of him.

My life was changing, I was a wolf now, but I was Redwood.

And as my mate wrapped her arm around my waist, I knew this was just the beginning. Even with the unknown coming, there was still so much to live for, to fight for.

I was Redwood, and I was just now learning what that meant.

# EPILOGUE


Kaylee


"I THOUGHT we were supposed to wait for you to see me until the mating ceremony," I groaned as I wrapped my legs around Jason's waist.

He grinned at me, kissed me hard again as his hands dug into my ass. He pumped in and out of me, his cock thick, stretching me tightly. He had his suit pants down below his very bite-able ass, and I had my dress hiked up around my waist. The fact that we were in my bedroom, my back against the wall, and both of us trying to be quiet as we fucked hard and way too quickly for our own good, just told me it was time for that damn mating ceremony to begin.

"I'll act surprised if you do."

"Just make it quick, come already."

"Ouch."

I rolled my eyes. "My brother is going to be through that door any minute. And he's already going to sense what's going on."

Jason froze and glared at me. "Stop talking about family members while I'm balls deep inside you."

I blushed, wiggled. "Sorry. Do continue."

He slid the lace of my dress down below one breast and popped a nipple into his mouth, sucking hard. I threw my head back, the sensation going straight to my pussy, as he fucked me harder against the door. Between the sounds of our breaths, the wet slickness, and the door banging, I was pretty sure the entire gang knew what we were doing. And I didn't care.

When he reached between us and flicked his thumb over my clit, I came, clamping down on him so hard I was afraid I was going to hurt him. I couldn't focus, couldn't breathe, couldn't see, but then he was groaning my name, filling me with his seed.

I clamped my mouth on him, needing to taste him, needing to just be with him. And when he finished we sat there, both of us panting. I grinned.

"I can't wait to do that after the mating ceremony."

"What? Is it going to be different? Because we're going to have to practice then. I like practice."

I patted my geeky mate's cheek and then kissed him softly. "We need to clean up."

"Fuck yes, you do," Conner growled from the other side of the door.

I groaned. "Oh my god, Conner."

"I didn't hear anything. My mate wouldn't let me inside to stop the two of you so we'd be on time. But seriously? People are waiting. I don't need to hear my sister having sex."

"Sorry about that," Romy, Conner's mate, called from the other room. "I swear we weren't in the house until we heard the exclamation from you both. Good job, Jason!" Romy said, with a clap of her hands, and I snorted.

Jason let out a groan. "You know, going from no family to this much family is a little bit much."

"Of course it is. I also cannot believe that my brother found his mate at the same time that I did," I said, as Jason lowered me to the floor. We cleaned each other up quickly, and I straightened my dress. Jason spent a particularly long amount of time making sure my breasts were where they needed to be. The sensation made my nipples even harder.

I glared at him. "I do not need to be turned on during our ceremony."

"I'm always turned on when you are around. Get over it." He pressed a kiss on my lips, then smacked my ass, and we walked out into the living room. Romy and Conner were there, both of them leaning forward to one another, kissing softly.

I cleared my throat. "Hey. Not on my couch."

"I promise we're not going to have sex on your couch," Romy teased as she stood up, pulling her mate, my twin brother, with her. "Come on. You look gorgeous."

"You look great yourself," I said.

I didn't know Romy that well, but we would have lifetimes together finding out who we were. I liked this woman for my brother. She took no shit, was strong, much stronger than she thought she was, and a beautiful member of our family.

And I had all Conner's secrets wrapped up tightly to give her, morsel after morsel. Conner was going to hate it, though he was doing the same with Jason, so really, he couldn't blame me.

We made our way outside, where all three of my parents glared at us before they laughed. Then the three of them began kissing, just softly enough that all of my siblings and I rolled our eyes.

Jason chuckled. "I still can't get over how young your parents look."

"We're all going to look the same age for a long time. That's just the way it rolls. Welcome to your new life," I said, then leaned into my mate.

"There's also a lot more people here than I was planning on," he said, and he reached up to move his collar away from his neck.

I turned to him, sliding my hand into his. "Just think about it as just us. Yes, it's our family circle, but it's also the Pack and the Talons. Riaz is here too, as is Chase."

He frowned. "Chase is the Aspen Pack Alpha, right?"

"He is. And he's new. He's been away for a while, having been hidden away or something like that, thanks to the former Alpha being a jerk and a sadist."

Jason opened his mouth to speak, and I shook my head. "I'll explain in detail later. Needless to say, Chase is here because he wants to learn how to be a decent Alpha and not like the asshole who raised him."

"So, in other words, we're in a political situation where we have to be on our best behavior?"

I shook my head and kissed him softly. "No. It's just us. Chase is here to learn and to celebrate. Same as Riaz." I smiled softly. "Our world is changing, everything is getting a little more intense, a little more scrutinized, but we're still here. I have lifetimes with you, Jason. To learn who you are, to learn who we could be. I can't wait to see exactly how your wolf acclimates to this new world of ours. And how strong he will be. I love you, Jason," I said, surprising myself.

His eyes darkened, even as they glowed slightly around the iris.

"I've been waiting for you to say that. I didn't want to be the weirdo that said it first."

I narrowed my eyes. "Are you calling me a weirdo, Jason?"

"Never."

And then he leaned forward and kissed me softly. I moaned into him. "I love you, Kaylee."

And then I smiled at my mate as everyone cheered around us.

The mating ceremony would begin in truth, and we would connect to the Moon Goddess and secure our Pack even more in its connection to the earth and to the magic that made us who we are.

But that would come later. For now, I held my mate and knew that no matter what darkness came, we would fight it together.

****

And next in the shifter world? I'm heading to the Aspen Pack with Etched in Honor! A certain cat shifter is waiting for her HEA

!

# A NOTE FROM CARRIE ANN RYAN

Thank you so much for reading **MATED IN DARKNESS!**

I LOVE writing this bonus romance. When I wrote Trinity Bound over ten years ago, I never thought I'd write the next generations' romance! I'm thrilled to be writing the Talon Pack series again!

And next in the shifter world? I'm heading to the Aspen Pack with Etched in Honor! A certain cat shifter is waiting for her HEA!

**The Talon Pack:**

Book 1: Tattered Loyalties

Book 2: An Alpha's Choice

Book 3: Mated in Mist

Book 4: Wolf Betrayed

Book 5: Fractured Silence

Book 6: Destiny Disgraced

Book 7: Eternal Mourning

Book 8: Strength Enduring

Book 9: Forever Broken

Book 10: Mated in Darkness

**The Aspen Pack Series:**

Book 1: Etched in Honor

**While you wait for more wolves, try the Ravenwood Coven series!**

**The Ravenwood Coven Series:**

Book 1: Dawn Unearthed

Book 2: Dusk Unveiled

Book 3: Evernight Unleashed

If you want to make sure you know what's coming next from me, you can sign up for my newsletter at www. CarrieAnnRyan.com; follow me on twitter at @Carrie-AnnRyan, or like my Facebook page. I also have a Facebook Fan Club where we have trivia, chats, and other goodies. You guys are the reason I get to do what I do and I thank you.

Make sure you're signed up for my MAILING

LIST so you can know when the next releases are available as well as find giveaways and FREE READS.

Happy Reading!

Want to keep up to date with the next Carrie Ann Ryan Release? Receive Text Alerts easily!

**Text CARRIE to 210-741-8720**

Carrie Ann Ryan is the New York Times and USA Today bestselling author of contemporary, paranormal, and young adult romance. Her works include the Montgomery Ink, Redwood Pack, Fractured Connections, and Elements of Five series, which have sold over 3.0 million books worldwide. She started writing while in graduate school for her advanced degree in chemistry and hasn't stopped since. Carrie Ann has written over seventy-five novels and novellas with more in the works. When she's not losing herself in her emotional and action-packed worlds, she's reading as much as she can while wrangling her clowder of cats who have more followers than she does.


www.CarrieAnnRyan.com